For all orders and enquires please contact the Author & Distributor: Carl Aabye at 1614 4th Ave south Fargo ND 58103 or carlaabye@yahoo.com

Publisher: Steele Publishing, United States

International Standard Book Number: 0-9701119-3-2

International Standard Book Number: 978-0-9701119-3-7

Printed in the United States of America

Foreword

Carl believes this story contains something of value to
be pondered or thought about. Moreover, Carl has serious concerns about the erosion of our civil liberties.
In addition, Carl understands why many feel the need
for security and reform.

To paraphrase: Do we have to give up our freedoms:
the tenants of our precious Bill of Rights to grasp for
attaining security?

Carl has a wide spectrum of knowledge about political
and religious thought, and he has spent many hours
studying reference material including the Minneapolis
Tribune; U.S.A. Today; The Wall Street Journal and
Carl also reads his hometown paper: the Fargo Forum
daily. Carl hoped to get a book review from the Forum
on his first book: *Terrorist among Us* but as he has
stated in the past, "It's hard to be a prophet in your
own home town."

Carl would like to thank everyone that participated in
this project: Kathy Mager, Michael J. Steele and
Mike Todd for editing and networking with me on the
excellent story line.

Carl wouldn't be surprised if you pick up on his North
Dakota and Red River Valley of the North Scandinavian influences.

Warning: I admit to a belated ego driven poor decision to do the cover,but I stress: That if you judge this book by the cover you're missing one hell of a story.

Side Bar: I wrote most of this in late 03 and early 04 and then seemed snake-bit to polish it off (Some may say left in the rough). I came across this the other day; it pertained to a magazine prescription. Pray tell what else is out there.

Please Note

August 8, 2006

Dear Subscriber:

Our bank has just informed us that because of the Patriot Act we may no longer deposit checks made payable to The Individual Christian Scientist or to T.I.C.S. even though we have been doing so for thirty years.

Checks must now be made payable to Doris… (I omitted her last name) C.A.

Thank you for your cooperation Doris.

Patriot Act ----- Gone Awry

Chapter One -- Futurist Birthday

Dads on my mind; he retired from work early and that became a problem for him, because I know that Dad still has a tremendous amount of energy left inside of him. For example, Dad attacks the Internet with the ferocity of a Keith Richards on guitar. I need a break from studying this early evening, so I am going to call my older sister who is soon expecting her third child around the same time of her upcoming 25th birthday.

I called her and she asked, "Well Junior, what are we planning for Dad's big 50th birthday next month?"

I answered, "Well sis, you still sure know me like a book."

Sis responded, "Junior, you're sweet but easy to read."

"Linda, Dad's birthday is on a Sunday this year so why not invite him out to a nice place for supper, and we could have a few of his friends just show up?" I heard her best laugh; she agreed and said, "We need to pin him down soon. You know since dad retired six months ago, he's now on some secretive project that has kept him busier than ever traveling all over God's green earth. Dad even went to some Malaysian city that sounded like Koala Bear to me."

Linda and I visit on the phone for another fifteen minutes or so, and after a few I love yous' we hung up. Soon thereafter, I started to seriously wonder what the old man has been up to all this time. I know he has received a lot of opinions on whether he should have retired early, and he was wondering what he should do with his time. True to form: Dad just shrugs his shoulders and smiles and says he is working on it. I remember he looked like a cottonwood seed hung up in the wind for about the first three months, but now he's like a hound that picked up the scent of something, and either he's too busy to tell us or he will in his own time. Friday has come, and it has been another nice winter so far. The past few weeks just flew by. Today, I'm looking forward to my last spring break as a graduating college senior in this year of our Lord 2003. In addition, I am looking forward for the short eighty-mile trip from Grand Forks, North Dakota to my hometown of Moorhead, Minnesota. I can't wait to practice swinging my elbow Saturday night before Dad's fair-sized party. Moreover, I'll also get to see Linda's little baby girl: the one that we are excited about being Linda had two boys before she had the little girl. We had a hard time trying to keep the guest list small since Dad is pretty popular, and I suppose next we'll get our ass chewed out royally for leaving out some good friends, and worse yet relatives from our surprise party because the place we're having it at isn't all that big.

The day before Dad's surprise party I make my way to

my hometown, and I even made plans to go out with some old buddies. I survived the bash, and as usual the sun just had to come up regardless this Sunday morning. Being young and dumb to some degree I manage to not get up until noon, and I am not any too bright eyed either. Around four P.M. I made necessary phone calls, and I anxiously wait to go over to Dads' to meet with Linda, her new baby, the boys, and her computer geek husband: Mark. I understand when we leave Dads' we will all be traveling to the party in the Wold's new three-seat, passenger van.

Suddenly, an idea hits me, and I call over to Linda's place," Sis I will drive right over to your house, and ride with you guys to Dad's."

When I arrive I run inside, and search out little Sarah. Gee, I forgot how small newborn's are, but what a little doll she is, blue eyes and black hair.

Junior, she'll probably have brown eyes in a few more weeks just like both her brothers eyes changed from blue to brown."

We talk for a good half hour and then leave for Dads'. On the way I ask to be let off by his rear alley because I just love going through the garage and then entering the trap door in the rear corner that leads to the tunnel that Dad and I dug back when we built our new three-stall garage, which is bigger in square footage than our old house. I recall how we had to fight city hall for a special variance to build the garage larger than our old house.

Soon afterwards, they let me off, and I walk the half block down our alley as my mind drifts back to that labor of love as a thirteen-year old. I can remember digging those fifteen feet of tunnel from the new garage, which led to the secret still that we found in a room under our back yard, which led from a secret tunnel that exited our old house's basement. I now think back farther too when I was eleven, and Linda and I spent a lot of our summers with Dad after his and Mom's divorce. I remember helping Dad move those old canning shelves from the back basement wall, and we discovered ten years ago now the tunnel that led us to the secret room under our back yard. Dad figured there were a few other houses around our State with secret rooms where moonshine whiskey was made in the 1920's during prohibition.

Well, I know how to quickly enter Dad's locked garage, and I soon begin opening the hidden trap door on my way to my old kid's hideout. The smell is familiar as I traverse down and toward our discovered room. The slight musty aroma just reinforces my priceless memories. I then feel for the door opening and turn on the light. We rewired the old one-time moonshine room. I check the small fridge for a beer. No luck, then I enjoy listening to everyone on the old bulky, almost always turned on 60's era intercom that we had installed six or seven years ago back when I was an impressed fifteen year old. The sound is a little faint and distorted on this refugee from some of Dad's rummage sale shopping, but if I just concentrate, I know that I can pick up quite a bit of their muffled conversation. I don't even hear my name mentioned. Then I spot something behind a poster. What the Hell, an old AK-47 semi automatic rifle! I pick it up and see its clip and all. It's fully loaded, and I believe it has possibly been customized to be a full automatic. I believe with my limited knowledge that it was probably illegal. I shake my head in wonder; man this is really out of character for Dad to possess; it truly confused me. I flop on the old single bed for old time's sake for a few minutes. Next, I get up and sneak into the basement of Dad's old house, and then I run upstairs, and come up behind our laughing Daddy and taped the top of his balding head. He let out a howl. Who said, middle age men can't jump?

Linda scowls at me, "God Junior you'll give Dad a heart attack."

"Well sis you saw me, why didn't you warn him then?"

Soon afterwards, Dad apologizes and said, "I am a little extra jumpy lately and remind me to explain to everyone about my wild speculations later on."

I reflect back, and I blare out, "Dad, not the birds and the bees again or some wild sex story since you and mom have been divorced over ten years now."

Dad laughed and said, "Scout's honor kids, it may well be more serious than a simple dose of the clap."

I even see my stiff brother-in-law Mark laughing a

little now, as if he's finally gotten used to our silly-loving- banter that a lot of people find weird. As grandma used to say, "Blank em if they can't take a joke."

We drive to the supper club and right after we're seated a real sweet young thing comes over by Dad in Marilyn Monroe style and starts gyrating as she straddles his lap while singing, "Happy Birthday, Carlie Baby." Next, a room divider opens up and a few more people that we invited start their video and digital cameras. Boy, I'm glad I always bring my digital camera with me as x-rated pictures could bring some good blackmail money. Linda and I shed a few tears as the group transitions into singing *He's a Jolly Good Fellow* and then the *Shores of Montezuma*. Even our reserved Dad had to grab some linen off the table to wipe away a few. The night is just a blast.

Around eleven P.M. a few people start saying their goodbyes to Dad. Finally only Uncle Ben is left besides our van full, counting sis's long sleeping kids; we agreed that everything had worked out just fine.

"Well, Daddy?" we said in unison, "we're ready to hear a story from the old master storyteller himself."

Dad began to tell us what his thoughts were, "That's exactly what I've been into lately, trying to tell a necessary good bow shot story."

Then he stood up and twisted his jaw and he spoke out:

You know, 9-11 got my mind a going and when I talked

about it in nausea or is it nauseous-ness, until their eyes started to glaze over, I felt I may be turning some people off, no matter how patriotic they are. You know I was highly decorated myself from my tour in Vietnam, but as I told you before we don't want to flaunt that old stuff. A lot of folks, you all realize, wonder why I retired so early. I've always tried to stay ahead of the curve and sometimes it works and well what the hell, all I know is when you are perceived as doing well, you're a genius and when your not, you're an idiot. I like to think I'm somewhere in between. I was real, real lucky to stupidly put a bit of money in only a couple high tech areas in the late 80s and a few thousand in Harley Davidson, right after the employee buy out, didn't hurt much either. Kids, maybe you shouldn't tell your mom how lucky I was.

We all have a good laugh with that confession. Anyway, to make a long story short, you know you're Granddad - my Dad lost some very hard earned money near the end of the twenties and we could see and hear his pain until the day he passed just a short seven years ago. In fact he urged me to cash out of the market before I did. I guess what finally made up my mind was after a fourth straight federal reserve raising of interest rates in a compressed time frame that ended up being six straight. I guess I thought someone was treading close to influencing an election or afraid of a bubble in the market getting bigger. Any who where were we?"

I yell out, "Dad, just what the hell is a loaded AK-47 doing in the dugout bedroom?"

Dad in a calming voice replied:

Jr. that's not the only one I've purchased, but I'll try and explain, so pay attention. I've probably avoided telling you my fear. I feel my very life has been threatened for a time now. I didn't want to needlessly worry you. But I had already resolved in my mind to tell you my concerns tonight. Let's see, I was just kind of bumming around after I first retired, well, that's what I told some people, but I was like a relaxed sponge, breathing a lot in. I also knew I needed some cardiovascular activity so I went to a local mall early mornings and walked and talked with some way older farts than I, and that walking seemed to just expand an imagination I didn't know I still possessed. Now getting real serious as I have your undivided attention, I don't think I'm imagining what's happening in my life now.

I'm confused and ask "What's happening Dad?"

Dad answered, "I see you're shaking your heads and I apologize if I am making this overdramatic; I feel a little stupid talking about it. The it is; I can hardly believe I would ever try writing a book."

We all laugh, including Dad, who is actually even getting a red face.

Dad began to explain:

Kids, I'm now hooked on research and trying to scribble about terrorism, in the past, present and possible future. I've tried, for instance, to get up close and friendly with different and varied Muslims, but had limited success because of their sensitivity. I even traveled to Dearborn and Detroit, and not our precious, nearby Detroit Lakes, Minnesota. But Michigan, which has a long time large Arabic presence; however, for the most part over time, even though they maintain much of their religion and culture they are now very Americanized"

Then I was steered to New Jersey and later, Florida. I was getting excited and even given places, persons and times to make contacts in Kuala -- Lumpur, Malaysia.

My curiosity got the best of me, and I asked, "Dad, let's see your passport."

He giggles and passes it around to us along with some neat pictures.

I made a quick comment, "Hey Dad, some of these women don't look too   bad."

Dad spoke on:

Jr., that turned out to be about the only plus. Actually the varied architecture and markets would have been real interesting if I wasn't so pissed off. I felt I'd been made a fool of because I couldn't make any contacts in that large sprawling city. I thought I was being watched, but I can only speculate by whom, they could have even been our C.I.A. for all I know .You know old Dad when he's got a burr under his saddle and needless to say, upon returning to the States and Florida I

confront those Arabs at a Florida pawn shop, for that
wild goose chase. Boy, did they come out of their
shoes and the woodwork. But by God, I had to start
backing water and made a hasty retreat. As I got in my
car that day and peeled off, I had noticed in my rear
view mirror, a group had run out behind me and was
taking video or pictures of my fleeing car, with my
Minnesota plates. During that time of panic, I can re-
member thinking back: I believed they had something
shiny in their hands. I couldn't believe that day all of
the filtering in of Sand Monkey's behind the cover of
the people closest to me.

I replied, "Come on dad, I know it will take
more than that to stop you, and like you and Gramps
often told me through the years, 'Damn the torpedoes
and full speed ahead."

Dad continued on explaining:

Thanks, but I now may try to keep a lower profile. I
even had an Arabic speaking friend try and decipher
some troubling background Arabic that my trusty
voice activated tape recorder had picked up that day.
In the recent past I had even spent a lot of time at our
local library, on the Internet, and read copious
amounts of information. I even read the Turner
Diary's and the Anarchist's Cookbook in my middle
age years, or should I say old age

Linda yells, "No dad, you're a very young 50."

Dad looks Linda in the eyes and states,
"Truthfully I am now so paranoid that I discontinued

my personal Internet service, and now I am using a close friend's if it's really necessary. I besides a couple AK-47 also purchased a couple small hand guns and feel somewhat naked tonight without my piece."

I continue with a question for dad, "Dad, have you a hidden permit or whatever to carry?"

"No son, I didn't even try for a concealed as it's almost impossible to get in our County."

Linda said, "Daddy, don't shoot yourself, we want to have a bigger 60th birthday party in ten years for you."

We revert to small talk but they still boot us out at one A.M. in the morning. The next day, I said my good-byes, and I am off to meet some of my buds for a long planned spring break trip at the beaches of Florida. The trip had been awesome. I survived the break and realized it was a good experience, but I needed to return to real life. The hangovers were debilitating! After a few more short weeks of hitting the books and ten days of way above average temperatures for late April and the beginning of May, I decide my friends back home in Fargo - Moorhead need me to justify their purchase of a sixteen-gallon keg of luscious draft beer.

The eighty-mile drive to the south flew by. I pull into Fargo - Moorhead at seven P.M. I find the party. I am going to try to pace myself as I've planned to have a sober- designated- female driver escort us uptown around ten P.M. for a grand tour of watering holes, after an hour and a half of warm up practice here at the party house. The weather this night must be a factor in the draft beer going down so fast and easy. I can't help but notice Julie: the petite younger sister of one of my best friends. She has added a few choice curves in appropriate places, and she has an extra facet or sparkle in her eyes. I know she always liked me and that's why she was given a chauffeur's cap so when we call on our cell phones she can pop into a bar or wherever and yell, "Your ride's here."

We are sociable this evening, recalling good stories, and were singing every song that one after another of us miraculously recall. Now at closing time our effervescent designated driver once again has the unenviable job of stuffing us silly, overgrown, obnoxious, and plastered young men into a thank- God- full sized van. Once back at the party location we polish off some more suds and around three A.M. I decide to drive over to Dad's so that I can crawl into my boyhood bed that is very comfortable. In addition, I love the cool environment. Besides a probable headache later in the morning will be more tolerable in that luscious cool dampness of the underground bedroom.

The cute designated driver: Julie said, "No Way."

Now, she starts reaching in both my front pockets for my car keys. I almost lose my balance in my state of stupor, but I am real aroused and am enjoying the hell out of this. "Julie baby you play rough for a young girl."

"For your information Carl Jr., just last week I went from no adult rights to complete rights on my eighteenth birthday."

"Damn it Julie, you got my keys."

Suddenly she throws them to someone, and then she grabs my long hair at the back of my head and kisses me a good one.

Later on, after coming out of a half-blackout, knowing how stubborn I am, after having a little more beer, I get my way and she drives me to Dad's. I guess she probably had her way with me a little earlier thanks to pure testosterone and youth overcoming inebriation to some uncertain degree. I do know that my wobbly legs are now weak and like rubber as she is on the short side. Can you imagine her taking advantage of me in my condition? And I bet she won't respect me in the morning either.

She doesn't look like a happy camper as she drops me off in our alley. I manage to navigate or wobble the half block walk down the alley to Dad's place. Even in the dark and in my condition, I still know how to easily enter the seemingly locked garage. I'm almost tripping over a couple items in the dark night and darker yet garage. I can't help it, but I've got a case of the shits and giggles. As I go down through the hidden trap door to the almost six-foot tall tunnel, I tell myself to get serious, so when I get to my underground respite, I won't wake Dad up as he might hear me through the crude intercom. I successfully navigate, turn a light on, and I could turn off the intercom but don't bother with that option. I flop on the hard, old single-sized hospital mattress and enjoy the insanity for a few seconds, as I drop off to an alcohol induced unconscious state of sleep.

Later on, still half asleep, my ears must have picked up on some unrecognized human voices. God Dad do you need to have your radio on?   I almost doze off again but the intermittent strange few words over the intercom force me to press my watch to check the time in this always-dark environment. I see it's almost ten A.M. as I get up and turn a light on and rub my rough gritty feeling eyes. I pick up a few more words and some very derogatory talk about Dad in the past tense that gets my heart rate from practically non-existent to full race in seconds. I try and calm myself and grab Dad's still loaded AK-47, while I   quietly as possible head for the main house. I tell myself to relax, as it's most likely nothing, but I'm primed to some degree because of what Dad's fears are, and I never even heard his voice once over the intercom. I hope these old basement steps won't creak too much as I sneak upstairs. Although I'd reseated a lot of the nails, and I had added a few sheet rock screws last summer. I had even oiled a few of our old door hinges. Dad, you are not the only Hanson that prepares for and anticipates the future. The dam gun wants to run into everything. Would I ever really use it? I enter the kitchen with all the stealth I can muster, and it sounds like they are just around the corner. I'm concerned they will hear my pounding full race heart and heavy breathing. I peer at the entryway to the dinning room or old doorway, which long ago had its door removed, and it is about three feet from the outside wall. I don't see anyone from this angle. I stretch my neck and realize they must all be more to the center of the next room. There is a large old buffet on one side of the doorway, and there is an easy chair on the other. I now get down on my one hand with my knees crawling forward until I can peek around the door opening by the buffet. There are three men approximately in their 40's and well manicured and dressed. I see from my level that they have some pretty tidy footwear. I'm relieved that they were all looking the other way when I had made my small target a moving object that possibly could have caught their peripheral vision. Now I wish I was standing up, and I had a better drop on um. Then, I would demand them to explain their presence while I call our police department. I sure miss my cell phone that I must have left in my car or the party last night as I try not to pull on the trigger.

One of the men said, "The place is clean and I left a couple goodies.

The other men are standing alongside Dad's computer, and one says he also added a gadget or two that would capture every future computer keystroke.

The third man said that he had finished scrubbing things while he was hacking the drives. He now closes his little suitcase that looked like it had some fancy stuff plus a laptop looking devise inside.

One of them mentions the court approved warrant for a G.P.S. on his car had been helpful, "Guess we don't have to worry our heads over Mr. Carl Hanson anymore, and I hope we don't get any more calls for mop up, scrubbing action."

They are still laughing when one repeats twice "they did get a warrant via a judge for the tracking device didn't they?"

My heart is beating faster yet if that's possible and I can feel it pounding in the top of my head. My mouth is super dry and it's more than last nights drinking. I notice they are all at least thirty-five, and they look and dress so much alike. Now one of the bastards starts to turn my direction. My God, he is pulling a gun out of some kind of a shoulder harness! I blast all three with Dads evidently modified full automatic!

God, the rifle had just jumped around in my hands with an almost slow motion effect, but mostly it is like a bad dream. I keep screaming at the top of my lungs as I tear around our small house and everything is in order, and thank you lord no Dad sighting here as I call out, "Dad, I'm home, it's me! Answer me please!" I look the men over for some ID's and find nothing, at least in my hurried frenzy, However, I see they had something I'm pretty savvy about, and they are wired. They have some fancy, highly sophisticated looking; I presume open microphones under their suit coats. I am operating under adrenaline, and I don't know why I took one of their pistols. Moreover, I still had my new digital timed camera. Feeling possessed I took a couple pictures. I have no idea why I even take their digital camera. In addition, I take a few more shots of this bloody gruesome scene. Now I run to see if Dad's car is parked out front like he often parks it this time of year. Thank God, no Daddy's car. A fast approaching car suddenly screeches to a stop. Similarly dressed men are getting out of a car that was still skidding to a standstill. I see one has drawn a pistol as they run this way, I panic and run for the back door. I think about exiting back through the tunnel, and like it down there but I sure as hell don't want to be shot down there. Perhaps, I might not be found for a while, so I drop in the kitchen the rifle that would slow me down and fly out the back door were I immediately ran across our neighbor's back yard at an angle until finally, I am in the next block's alley. I ran the alleys for two blocks until I have to turn north or south. As I turn and glance back, I hope I'm just imagining this but I think I just saw the very back end of Dad's red car disappear from view as if entering our garage. I'm bewildered, and I don't know which way to turn or what to do. If I had my cell phone I believe I would likely call 911. I decided to right or wrong walk to where my car was parked. I somehow at least had gotten my car keys back. What a time for my mind to now be flooded with great flashbacks of Julie. God, I now think about her reaching one arm back behind me and pulling as if she could get me any closer to her. What clenching and wild gyrations that young goddess performed. I also now remember setting her on the bathroom sink, but had to stop because I sensed it was about to tear off the wall of my friend's apartment. Maybe my brain will stop spinning out of control long enough to work out some sort of a game plan. As I walk along I hear some sirens and my poor overworked heart starts pounding out of control again. I just keep on walking and am amazed I still have their pistol and camera stuffed in my pants pockets. I hope and pray Dad's okay. I just can't make heads or tails of this. It's like a bad dream or a television rerun of an old Ron Sterling episode of the *Twilight Zone*. I have a lot of faith in Dad being able to take care of himself, and I know when I shot those men they were in our castle. Dad always said if you shoot someone robbing our house and they get outside to pull him or her back in, so if they check out early from life they are in the house. I also thought the one saw or heard me, and I just re-acted to what I thought were men who talked like they just killed Dad. It again comes back to me that I'd never pulled a trigger on a full automatic and it felt like it was going to jump right our of my hands. It seems that all of my luck today has been bad, but I see my car is still where I left it. I quickly take off and turn my car radio to A.M. like I am on some sort of Autopilot. I next locate an ATM machine, and I almost empty my account.   I'm thinking about going the route of a temporary fugitive with at least a small degree of independence until this whole mess sorts itself out. I buy some food, writing paper, envelopes, and stamps. Next, I decided to drive to the temporary sanctuary of an actual wildlife sanctuary that our family had traversed and hiked often years ago. In less then an hour and a half I arrive at the edge of the Tamarack Wildlife Refuge where it's as pristine and alive as ever. There are a lot of small lakes, streams, slews, and what have you. This tranquil reserve was probably established as a waterfowl reproduction area. I have a hard time in this area getting the 6:00 P.M. hometown local T.V. news that's also on the radio. I get bits and pieces, and tomorrow I'll travel out and locate our local newspaper. I was going to try the radio again at 10:00 PM but fell asleep in the car. I wake up pretty early, and I devour a can of cold pork and beans mixed with a craving I had for some cottage cheese. I really like the two mixed together, and I finished off the large container of cottage cheese, as I know it won't keep long this time of year with out refrigeration. I find my cell phone under the car seat but it's possibly good that the battery is getting old and had gone dead. I had wanted to call Linda, but I decided to wait until after I find out what's going on, or just maybe I won't dare call anyone. I guess I really don't know much, and I hit the temple part of my head with the heel of my hand and yell, "Wake up Carl! Wake up DAM IT!" God I hope Dads okay!"

I drive these pristine back roads with dense pine trees on both sides that are interrupted by a few open meadows, some lowlands and small beautiful lakes. I stop at an old historic site that has Indian burial sites on both sides of the road.

The west side predates the east site, and it has mounds where they were buried sitting up with I believe some possessions at ground level. I believe these were Dakota or what ever they called themselves before the French later began referring to them as the Sioux tribe. I have heard speculation that the French translated their Ojibwa and Cree scouts derogatory names of the Dakota or Lakota Indian Tribes into the French equivalent word Sioux. I walk back to the East side where my car is parked and marvel at the casket-size birch bark and wood houses that with no disrespect remind me of long dog houses that were laid over the body facing west. There was a small hole at the west end so the soul could travel in a few days across the plains then the mountains and on west to the ocean. This is the Ojibwa later mispronounced by the new settlers as Chippewa tradition, and it makes practical sense to me as our lifeless bodies return to Mother Earth. I see a soaring eagle, and it's nice to know that the eagle population has really been making a comeback. To me it's a symbol of the regenerative powers of nature and man in cooperation for a change. I always enjoy the different smells in the air that stir the memory as I reluctantly leave this sanctuary. I drive through small to medium size resort area towns that must at least double in size during the summer. I think to myself that it's not even calendar summer yet. Maybe the summer like weather just brought in more car traffic from the bigger cities. I travel to a small café where I know they have homemade or made at the site pies and pastry. I order just plain banana bread that is not heated up and butter with coffee. I dig through some already read newspapers that were left behind to find our hometown daily. I've got Dad on the brain, and I recall him telling me a lot of newspapers years back ran a morning and evening edition. If that was Dad's car I saw, and if anything happened to him I won't be able to live with it. I sit down and it's a good thing. There at the bottom of the front page is a somewhat vague response to what is to me personally another twilight zone like major event.

Before I can even move my riveted eyes to read, my mind keeps repeating: why did I not call our local police before leaving town as if a fleeing guilty person? After all, I was justified in doing what I did when I felt my life was going to be taken in my own Dad's house! Wasn't I? Then I take a deep breath, and attempt to read and comprehend. As I read I discover that apparently there's a lid on the unfolding story.

They more or less apologized and said more will come out as the federal government is in the process of taking over jurisdiction, and the U.S. Attorney General is actively formulating a course of action. Future announcements in this case are a matter of National Security, and they have a need for some anonymity in this very fluid continuing event and investigation.

I read some off the record information from an anonymous source that relayed their opinion or whatever to a newspaper reporter. He or she comments that there will soon be confirmation and names of three FBI agents who were ambushed and fatally shot while performing a necessary and now legal action under the Patriot Act. A post 9-11 action in gathering information that could prevent future acts of terrorism by suspected terrorists. The reporter reiterates that this is off the record information they had diligently gathered and that the justice department will likely detain the alleged as a military combatant. Moreover, the local long time resident will likely be detained at an undisclosed location. The correspondent then goes on that they can verify that John Johnson: a prominent local attorney is quite adamant that he can't even get access to the alleged perpetrator, In addition, he strongly vouches for his character as a good loyal citizen that also had valiantly served his Country as a past U.S. military man who incidentally is a decorated combat hero. I guess there will be more to follow and that's an understatement. Thank you Lord that Dad's alive, and

I'm partially relieved even as they hold him. Our house is now a crime scene, and it will be gone over with a fine toothcomb. They will be real curious about access to Dad's house. I'm sure they have talked to Linda and scores of other people. They most likely now have court approved phone taps on whom; I can't even venture to guess.

I'm thinking about casing the car lots or mechanic shops; anyplace I can find a vehicle that has current license plates where the vehicle looks out of service. I have a need to borrow the plates off a just 'standing around' vehicle. Then I'm probably going to drive down to Missouri to send a letter to Dad's and Linda's addresses telling them I am on my way to old Mexico with some drug running friends I just met (they have some great wheels). I'm just along for the ride and unique learning experience. I'll add "P.S. Don't worry, Love You, Junior. Then after my diversion tactics I will back track, and travel up to a northern Minnesota resort by the Canadian border that a college acquaintance: Chad Teigan's parents own. I respect and like him. He previously invited me to his folk's place. Chad is a law student who's going to work there this summer. I'm already planning in my mind a public relations campaign to try to fuel pressure and public opinion for Dad. I only hope and pray that will cause some misstatement by our; I'm so agitated right now; I won't even say to myself what I'm thinking! Ambushed my ass, please dear God help me, help us! As I leave the restaurant my nerves are a little jumpy, and I didn't even drink that much coffee. I try to tell myself that I am now on a mission to right some egregious wrongs to our civil liberties. We're in the right so try to stay cool, and I am only retreating to regroup for the continuing battle. I'm not a runaway fugitive, but no matter my internal pep talk, I feel like one. I soon spot some suitable license plates. I park a couple blocks away and walked back with a few basic tools that I thankfully always carry in my cars. It's broad daylight and I like that as I've convinced myself that these new plates are mine, and I act accordingly.

I decided to purchase a fairly broad brimmed hat. I drive along on a old U.S. two-lane highway that meanders to the south. I put my inside window visors down a bit to keep the interior light down if even just a little. I feel the old two-lane will have less law enforcement, and the angle of oncoming traffic will be reduced as in my somewhat paranoid state I visualize that my likeness and thank goodness common car may be out there on some list; even if there isn't an official all point bulletin specifically looking for me. I drive along questioning everything I'm doing. Maybe this trip is an unnecessary risk but this whole nightmare is new territory for me. Killing three men: F.B.I. agents and having them hold my Dad for it is mind-boggling! I've got to quit thinking negatively. I am oblivious to the sights and miles as I come to the conclusion that I've got to lay in the weeds and not overplay my hand, as right is might, and Dad's a good man, and he will have an important support system behind him.

I just intend to be a fly in the soup and I am going to try against all odds to get them in a checkmate or make his unconstitutional detainment more of a negative than a positive. In my now self-induced, upstage mood, I utter out loud: "Hell man, ambush my ass, I'll show you ambush!"

I have no worldly idea why I think I need to get to Missouri to send a letter back home. I know it's the 'Show me' State. One of Dad's hero's Harry Truman lived and retired there after his Presidency. I can vividly see Dad strutting around the house with Granddad and one or the other saying, "Give 'um hell Harry!" and the other mimicking President Truman and pronouncing, "I don't give 'um hell, I just tell the truth and they think its hell."

When I was a small boy Gramps used to have fun making me laugh while he was having fun waving a newspaper around and imitating Truman, who was in turn imitating an apparently well-known radio commentator of that time, who had a distinctive delivery. I vaguely remember it was about a prematurely mistaken newspaper headline that some Mr. Dewey defeated him.

I'm now approaching the Missouri border. Oh—oh did that oncoming Highway Patrolman just drop his jaw? He is tapping on his brakes. I don't know but I floorboard it up this big hill, and then on the downhill,

I suddenly decide to dynamite my brakes to turn onto a side road. I brake into a sweat as I turn into a small store parking lot. It wasn't much more than a minute when I see flashing lights from the highway zoom by in the direction I had been traveling. My dam radio can't seem to hold a station in this area but now manages to play an oldie: *Don't Worry Be Happy.*

I somehow take a power nap, and then tentatively drive southwest to get closer to Interstate 29 to find my first town of size. I stop and wrote similar letters to Dad and Linda, and drop the letters into a mailbox. I'm glad my mind had cleared enough to think of also writing her. I turned my car around, and I feel more comfortable driving back toward the scene of the crime. I believe it's a crime, in a sense all right. On the way back, my mind is active, and I try to recall words I had heard over the intercom. I remember something about files and that one of them may have been called Python. Also a reference to a G.P.S. that I believe stands for Global Positioning System which was perhaps attached to theirs' or Dad's car. It could quite possibly be something of great importance. Things Dad told me years ago drifted in and out of my mind. Things like, "Son, don't strive for money but strive for excellence, and you most likely won't have any money problems." I sure am going to strive for justice and success if that's possible, Dad.

Before I realized it I'm back at the southern Minnesota border and consider taking a different set of roads that will eventually get me northeast of where I am. I want to stay focused so I make a conscious effort to avoid the news and newspapers for now. When I'm hopefully settled in and holed up, I'll gather up all I can get my hands on. Then I hope I can still keep the faith and take care of business. It is all I can do to keep from just calling up and saying, "Let Dad go, come and get me, I did it. I can prove it with my timed digital camera." I guess there's always that possibility later if I can just maintain my patience and stay disciplined, and discipline is sure not my strong suit, but self-preservation is something that I am good at. I guess it's obvious my fingerprints will be all over the AK-47 and also all over the house for that matter. I guess even some from a few weeks before this unfortunate incident. It sounds as if, thank God, Dad's being held, but at least alive. It's beyond me how they could actually charge him, let alone ever convict him?

My God I don't think he will get a day in court!

I thought to myself, "Well Carl, keep your mind on driving, as you didn't slow enough for that last sharp curve in the road."

I'm lucky in a sense that I look like a lot of people my age, and I am quite average with only being a little on the high side as for height and weight. I also have no visible unusual tattoos, moles or anything like that. I'm also a little more ruggedly handsome than the average. No brag just facts, and I still have some of my cockiness about me, and I haven't shaven for three days. I see my beard has more red hair in it than I realized. I think I'll just let that sucker grow as I at least think it disguisingly interesting. I see resort signs, so it must not be too much farther. I've thought about it, and I decided to risk calling Chad, who is back in Grand Forks, by way of a pay phone. Chad should be at his dorm pad at this late afternoon hour of; my gosh it's seven P.M .I'm confused as I haven't slept for more than half hour power naps for quite a spell. Thank God, he answered his phone, "Boy, I'm glad your home Chadwick."

Chad nervously spoke, "Carl, I'm just becoming aware of your Dad's situation but talk to me, as I'm more of a listener than a talker."

I hinted, and he picked up that I didn't want him to acknowledge hearing from me, and I didn't want to say too much right now. I started using an alias and told him that I sure could use a reference up here in his north woods and lake country.

Chad asked questions and he talked about our short term future:

Carl or what's your new handle, Tommy Thompson? I will call my parents right now and set up room and board for you, plus you will get a small stipend to live on. I am about ready to graduate from Law School but as you know I promised my folks one more season of help. I will enjoy working with you shortly. My upcoming law school degree may serve as a real testament in the future.

We laughed a little and ended our conversation. I feel just tingly inside now, and I treasure that old thing about a 'friend in need is a friend indeed. I also appreciate he could read between the lines pretty well. I guess if Dad's friend a Lawyer can have the handle Johnny Johnson, I can be Tommy Thompson. I drove around and observed the beautiful lay of the land around the area with all these pristine glacial lakes. I put off for a good hour my entrance to meet Chad's parents. I finally got back somewhere near the resort area after trying to take a navy bath of sorts at a gas station. I finally had the precise location after asking quite a few people that had been out doing spring yard work at their summer cabins. That small gas station with a few basic staples must have been a good fifteen miles away from Chad's parents spread.

Upon my arrival I knock on the door and they both invite me in. She says, "You must be Tommy then, Chad called and gave us a heads up about you."

I don't know what to say, then his dad says, "We could a used you yesterday and the day before that even."

Then we shake hands, and I felt that the ice has been broken. Moreover, I feel they're really great people. We visit a little, and Chad's' mom can see that I was in need of a good nights sleep.

She leads me to a nice little cabin and says, "It's not much but I hope you'll like it."

I gratefully reply, "That's an understatement sweet lady."

Chad's mom continued, "You can call me Stella and come over for coffee and a light breakfast at seven A.M. if you want. Then you and dad can get started on my big to-do list."

I locate an old wind up alarm clock and set it. One nagging thought is on my mind, Chad's Dad reminds me of Jed Clampett, and the good sized Jethro Bodine ties in with Chad. I need to somehow wipe that darn cable rerun from my thinking. Now I recall how Dad and gramps claimed they got more of a kick out of reruns of Sanford and Son now than years back when it was on network television.

I hope to soon be in the arms of Morphine. I think my Dad's mom meant Morpheus or something or another. My other Grandma used to say, "Sleep tight and don't let the bed bugs bite." I don't know why these trite little things now seem so important to me in my some-what isolated world. Boy, a bed hasn't felt this good in a while, but then I guess it's been a fair spell. "Well, shut up Carl and sleep fast."

Morning's dawns, and I'm still a little groggy, but the coffee should help and I think some good old fashion work will do me wonders.

Jim and I grab Stella's list, and we start off to do chores; then she yells, "Chad said he was coming up for the weekend to see us, and remember forenoon lunch will be on the table at 10 a.m. sharp if her in-spection passes."

I hit if off good with Chad's dad, and I told him that

Stella was my Grandmothers name.

Jim replied, "Oh Tommy for the first 20 years we were married I didn't know she didn't like her given baptismal first name of Johanna, and she used Stella her middle name."

Now he's just smiling as we struggle to get some more boatlifts correctly placed in the still cold water.

Jim said remember, "Ten in the morning sharp and we will be sitting in Stella's kitchen for some cookies and milk."

I give Stella the grandest compliment, "These are just like my Grandma's sour cream cookies."

She said, "You betcha, and we both use the real stuff I'm sure."

I soon asked Stella if I could read the paper that she said she just picked up at the mailbox.

Stella answered, "No problem sonny, you just be prepared to move out when you see me swinging my broom."

Jim said "It's not so bad as long as she's not riding it." In a flash she grabbed the broom and whacked Jim a good one on the shoulder, and I saw her still flashing eyes. Then just as fast they hugged and giggled like some young kids. I'm thinking this must be like a window back in time of seventy years or so in some ways.

I glance at yesterday's newspaper with one eye as I watched Stella with the other. Nothing new except the Feds have now taken over full jurisdiction, and they are tight-lipped except in mentioning the possibility of the alleged being a material witness. I guess I don't understand that legal term and I need to touch base with Chad about it. One encouraging piece of news is that due to local pressure, they will be giving a short explanation of why the suspect is in custody, and they will officially release his name even though it's already widely known. The rest of the day and the next couple of days go by quickly. It's like a slice of heaven around here.

This evening I'm looking forward to Chad's homecoming tomorrow morning. Then speak of the devil, I see him walking over to my cabin. He has a million questions for me, and I excitedly ran off at the mouth as he writes some things down. He, like the lawyer he will become says that at least he's not officially in any jeopardy, which is of record, but he assumes there would be something prejudicial toward him, and this could bring about a new career direction, but he is only in it for the love.

Tom breaks into conversation, "Carl, oh excuse me Tom, I had considered taking my board exam to practice law, but now I'm not sure as I would then have obligations as an officer of the court. Although Tom, as your official Attorney we would also have client attorney rights of confidentiality or privilege."

I agreed, "Alright Chad, now after telling me how important it is for me to recall and tell every little snippet, tell me what you're holding."

Chad being a near professional now interrupted me:

Now Carl, or excuse me, I need to get used to referring to you as Tom, and your request, well that's a horse of a different color. Something of great importance, even if wrong, is that they have their man, your Dad. Now let me feel your forehead. Just as I suspected you must be off your rocker from a high temperature or some other disorder, but I think I will ignore your hallucinations and just humor you until you come back to your senses.

I realized that Chad the lawyer was correct, "Good thinking Chad, but what is this about Dad possibly being a material witness?"

Chad hypothesized, "Well Tom, I can speculate that's either confusion or a planned leak. Have you seen today's newspaper?"

I answered, "No, a little of the one day late mailed, yesterday's and I'm nervous as I suppose my limited support system is going to hit me alongside the head." Then Chad pulls a rolled up few pages of newspaper out of his back pocket. Wow, there's a picture of me, and a story to go along It states as the only son of my now infamous widely known Dad, they would like to touch bases with me on a couple of matters that could help my Dad as well as putting this serious matter in order. I like to condense or Para-phrase a bit for my own levity. From the start of the article clear to the end it stresses that I'm not a suspect.

I questioned Chad, "Then Chad if I'm not a suspect I can call my sister without fear of impunity."

Chad laughs and says,

*Please don't talk to your almost council as if a layper-
son. We know some people would be here in a heart-
beat, although it would possibly be good for Mom and
Dad's business, as I'm sure you've found out why I
treasure them. Tommy, then again they aren't quite
perfect as they are also seven days-of-work-a-week
people, and I've given up on changing them.*

I asked Chad for some clarity, "Chad, you mean like a
judge that told a seventy-year-old prostitute that was
before him for the umpteenth time that in her case he
sees little chance for rehabilitation? Well by the con-
torted look on your face, you at least seem to think
that's interesting."

The conversation continued, whereas Chad continued
questioning me, "Tom do you have any pictures of
your sister or other people of trust? Also shopping pat-
terns, churches, stores, restaurants, or anyplace they
are likely to visit?"

I immediately began to write out on paper everything
that I can think of, and I even asked Chad if I could
write Linda a personal note. He said I could, but he
had to censor it to protect me from any possibility of
putting myself in any sort of additional jeopardy.
Chad articulated his innermost feelings towards the
whole situation:

*What I'm learning is troubling enough, and it is a
conflict for myself and my future profession, but it's a
double-edged sword and as long as your not an offi-*

cial fugitive I will assist you, and in a sense, all of us. Tom, I'm talking about all citizens and their trampled civil rights. Remember this; Ben Franklin said those that give up freedom for security will end up with neither or something like that."

I questioned Chad's recollection, "Come on now Chad, if you're my mouthpiece or whatever, I expect you to know that stuff verbatim and wasn't that Thomas Jefferson?"

Chad the inquisitor continued, "Carl, or Tom, or whatever the hell your name is, for the record, it is near verbatim. Forgive me for asking this, but what would you have done if one or more of those FBI good guys, or break and entry crooks, or assumed assassins of your Dad, had survived your initial volley of self defense shots?"

I haltingly replied, "Damn you Chad, did you have to bring up one of my nightmare scenarios! I've thought about that many times. More than likely I would have called 911 for an ambulance and, and if I would have found Dad dead or dying in our house, well, -- I would have emptied the whole clip on them or smashed their skulls in with the butt of Dad's rifle!"

Chad spoke some sense to me:

Tom, I do agree with you that we need to try and mount a vigorous grass roots public relations battle to counter the immense advantage that they have in giving out information, spun or not. Tom, write down anyone you think might write an editorial to newspa-

pers that will paint a picture of the fact your Dad was

a good man attempting to gather information for a

book that could help our country in its continuing

struggle against terrorism. Also, the fact your Dad is

for us, not against us, as the President stresses. And

you probably caught the fact I said might, as in make

your list large, as a lot of supportive and sympathetic

people won't stick their neck out, because of real or

imagined fears that you and I couldn't began to under-

stand. Tom my blood pressure is way up now, but if we

can pressure them, I believe someone will possibly lie,

as I believe they already have! We have a few aces in

the hole and this will and must not stand!

Then I just break down, as I again think about the men

and their families. I apologize to Chad who looks vis-

ibly shaken. I blabber between sobs that I had glanced

at pictures of the men in the newspapers, and I had

even brought that part of the newspaper here to the

cabin, but I couldn't bring myself to read the articles

about the agents, their families or let alone their obitu-

aries. I try to stop my uncontrollable sobbing but my

uncooperative diaphragm keeps jumping, and I am

embarrassed by some of the sounds that escape me

against my best efforts.

I questioned Chad once again for some reassurances,

"God Chad, why did I come home that night and

sneak in the house like a juvenile? Look at the night-

mare tragedy for Dad, our family and other families."

Then Chad comes over and hugs me and pats my

back, and said,

I know you have feelings even if a stoic Scandinavian. Tommy just let it out and this whole bigger than life situation needs the cleansing of sunshine. Tom, the whole dirty truth needs to come out, and we are playing the highest of stakes hand for you and all that one man, or one case can represent, and God help us play it well. Carl, I guess I need to, until this matter is resolved, try to get in the habit or thinking of you by your new alias. Tom, this conversation makes me realize that if we can get some cracks in their foundation and keep pounding, as this matter will demand, and at some point, bring in bigger guns, because this unfortunate incident we both realize is way over our heads."

I asked Chad another serious question, "Chad, with their power couldn't they easily cover up or deny any and everything?"

Chad articulated his feelings:

Tommy, I expect a cover-up as a likely scenario, but they don't know what you observed or heard, or your digital camera with the precise time of day captured. I will be making copies' of your date specific time of day, digital pictures and put their government issued pistol away for safekeeping. I speculate they may have had surveillance cameras taking images of your Dad's rear and front house entrances for a week, and possibly saw the back of your head and body at a minimum as you bolted out the back door that fateful day, at

what ever precise time. I'm planning to contact a
trusted retired attorney, and a sharp College Law Pro-
fessor who is so surrounded by people and students
and ironically tunnels that he could drive the F.B.I.
nuts trying to determine any of his present or future
contacts. Speaking of tunnels lets lighten up, and tell
me more about yours, Tom?

I think to myself, I need a change of subject. I have
withheld from Chad the fact I had taken The F.B.I.
man's digital camera, but ditched it in the Tamarack
Game Refuge, because of my paranoia that they could
somehow trace my location by it.

Courtesy *Popular Science*

Chapter two--Miller's Cave

An intimate conversation continues on between Chad
and me.

Chad asked, "Tom, speaking of over our heads, I'm
wondering what keeps your backyard from caving in
on your tunnel, or underground room?"

I replied:

*Chad, you said something that reminds me that Dad
called the whole underground complex Miller's Cave.
I asked Dad why he called it that, and he said that is
an assignment for me if I wanted to know why. So I
dug, no pun intended, and I came up with an actual
cave in Georgia by that name where I wasn't too crazy
to learn had people lost in it? Dad just laughed when
I told him what I came up with and said "good for you
son," but he was mostly thinking if I would listen or as
a last resort make a request from Saturday and Sunday early morning local radio stations that feature old
country western music, so I could hear a country legend, and sing it to him for some trivia bonus points.
Dad told me the singer is one hell of an unheralded
guitar player, as well as having many big vocal hits,
and was originally from eastern Canada.*

Chad responded, "Tommy, I know the song and the
now deceased artist. Keep digging on."

I thought about it and said, "Well, let's be fair here,
you want me to tell you about Millers Cave? I'll be a

good sport, Chad, even if you're holding out on me to go along with your want to be lawyer mentality. Dad speculated by the ventilation and age of the house that the tunnel led to our Still, from back in prohibition days".

Chad gave me his advice, "Tom it's not a fair world. I need to see all your cards, but how I play them may sometimes be best confidential."

I wasn't in the mood to continue to communicate on a one-way street basis, but my big mouth won out, and I told him how Dad marveled at the engineering of the underground complex and their choice of long lasting building materials.

I further explained to Chad,

The sidewalls had a few extra, probably unnecessary railroad tie vertical timbers and a roof of cypress planks that do shrink and expand some depending on moisture but are still unbelievably sound. Dad discovered some tar paper from above, and he became curious if the whole thing was once dug from the top down, and he wondered if the workers filled it in afterwards, and if not, if one man could have possibly constructed it, as he most likely needed more hands than two. Also, as you leave the basement you step over the footings and down a good foot away it holds at least a foot of water in the tunnel, in theory at least, before water would run into the basement. Although we know water always seeks to the lowest level, however it can get there. Before Dad and I discovered the entryway in our basement behind the old canning shelves, Dad wondered about a drywell in the middle of our backyard and its sidewalls that came up a couple feet. Everyone thought it was cute and decorative. The people he bought the house from showed him how at times of continual high precipitation it could be pumped to dry out any unwanted groundwater, and it was a good ten-foot deep. It also turned out to aid or performed a ventilation task for the distilling process. . Before we found Miller's Cave he had considered filling the drywell because of possible liability concerns. Dad and I did add a heavy wire mesh to keep kids or animals from falling in. Although there is now a crude cover, it might not be adequate for an enterprising child. Dad would have loved to find out more, without making a big deal out of it or compromising our find.

Chad understood the historical significance of what I had explained to him and he said, "I understand. Tom, and with the passing of time there's likely no one left to ask."

I agreed, "You're exactly right on that. Chad."

Chad continued to speak:

Tom, those old timers could do some amazing things. I know when my Dad first bought this resort in the 60s and was adding some new water lines, a local legend, about 90, would just shake his head and explain how years back he would just go out in his back wood lot and hand auger eight foot length wood stock for water lines. My Dad just shook his head at that thought.

Then the old boy asked my Dad, "Where do they mine the metal for your pipe, Jim? How far do they ship to smelt it? How far away is the charcoal or lime rock or whatever they need to process the ore? Then how much more shipping goes on before the final processing into pipe and then shipped back to the user?" Dad just started to scratch his head and the old boy then asked Dad, "Where's your milk come from, the grocery store?" Then the rumpled old gent went into a far out story, that there are wood water pipes buried under ground in England that are still functional and used, or could be today after five hundred years and they only have to make sure the water pressure is held to certain limits, so go figure Tom.

It's now become late and Chad prepares to leave. I give Chad a sense of my gratification towards him and I say, "Chad, I'm thankful they must have received a quite old picture from Sis that had hit the newspapers, and I suppose also television screens. It is so old, rough and out of date that I almost didn't recognize myself."

Chad said as he walked off that he would personally be making those important contacts this week while coordinating with Linda and Uncle Ben for our own propaganda or public relations battle. Then I listened to the radio as I prepared to go to bed for the night. A weather report warns of possible severe thunderstorms in the next few hours for this part of the region. I thought, gee, it's early in the year for thunderstorms, but I would enjoy the sights and sounds, as it's been many months now since the last one. Then thoughts went way back to when mother would get Linda and me up in the middle of the night back when Dad was out of town on business, because she was afraid of the electrical storms that were accompanied with thunder. I was in grade school, and I thought she was silly, but I actually enjoyed those pajama parades around the house. I must have finally drifted off to sleep, and I even forgot to turn the radio off. I woke up for some reason and pressed my watch. I see its 2 A.M. I got out of bed, and I shut off the radio.

I looked out a window at the distant sky to check for lightning strikes. I hadn't heard any thunder, not even the distant type. Also, the ground still looks dry. I'm now startled as I see what I believe to be a medium blue colored dash light in a vehicle behind my car. I move back a couple feet from the window. My trusty barometer-like heart starts to pick up the pace again. I concentrate my vision in that area where I make out a black or dark colored vehicle. My thoughts are that some authority is checking out my vehicle or my borrowed plates, and I'm kicking myself for not ditching my wheels. I envision myself being taken into custody by a large group of law enforcement officials. Should I make a run for it now before there's more of a law enforcement presence? Wild paranoia takes over; maybe that is what someone hopes I do. I froze, just standing there staring out the window for a good half an hour. In my state of mind I am incapable of a plan B. I now see a police car pull along the dash-lit vehicle. After about fifteen minutes, the marked car drives away, and then suddenly a white suburban type sheriff's vehicle drives up. It in short order drives away. Not long after that happened, the first dash lit vehicle swings around and leaves. I felt a little relieved, and after another few agonizing moments I cautiously exited forth from behind the cover of some young full pine trees. As I slowly moved ahead my heart nearly stops. I caught the front fender and the tire area of a car as it turned around. It is standing about six hundred feet away, as if my mind giving me room to run for it but I scamper right back towards my cabin.

I hope they didn't see me. I am now quite shaken and my mind is running wild. I talk to myself, don't panic, as I remember what had happened the last time my reactions took over. I think about how upbeat I had allowed myself to get, as I felt we had a positive plan of action to bring justice for Dad, at least. My stomach and gut are reacting to my stress, and I wouldn't even dare flush the toilet as I imagined that any sound could be heard for twenty miles in this silent sanctuary that now imprisons me. I can't take this hemmed in feeling and wonder what they are waiting for. I half expect a wrecker from some distant location coming to haul off my getaway car. I stupidly imagine some fast asleep wrecker driver being summoned for a tow at this somewhat remote location at 4 A.M. and my heightened state of mind isn't painting pretty pictures. I decided that I am going out a window that faces another direction. I walk thru the woods as quietly as I can with every breaking twig thundering in my ear. Soon I am over by an elderly couple's place that Jim had told me about. I proceed on not even knowing why or where I am going. I freeze in my tracks again as there is yet another marked law enforcement vehicle parked a relatively short distance from me. They must be everywhere but it seems strange that they aren't in undercover or unmarked cars. This night is surreal and torturous.

I decide piss on it, I am just going back to my cabin, and I am going to go straight to bed. I feel like relieving myself by putting my back against a large tree, but the way my churning stomach feels; I would be concerned with the wind direction, and there's law enforcement everywhere. Maybe even out in the nearby lake.

Soon I crawl back in my window, and I fell asleep even though, I get up every hour to look out to see if my car is still here. Soon it's time to get up for work.

Chad comes over looking full of vigor and says, "What's the matter, aren't you awake yet?"

I told him, I didn't feel so hot and why."

Chad tries to keep a straight face as he tells me his Dad had apparently been called about 1:30 A.M. to keep an eye out for a local boy who was a suspect in a robbery of a near by lake resident's beer supply. They told Dad that the property owner held onto one of the two for a period of time and that He had recognized both of them. Moreover, the one that pulled away from the cottage owner was later recaptured, but they were still trying to locate the other sixteen-year old.

Chad recognizing that I was tired said, "I'll tell Dad you deserve a day off from time to time so that way you can sleep in some more this morning. I'll also write down some locations of people that will give you a few bucks to part your car out. You can do that later today if you survive that long as you look like warmed over death, there Tommy."

I didn't have enough energy to argue with Chad, and I just shook my head in an affirmative way. Chad said he was taking a couple days off, and that he might even see my sister Linda and her husband: Mark in church later on. He also suggested that they would set up an effective old-fashioned way to communicate. I asked what that would be and Chad replied, "Tommy that is not for you to worry about, as you will be busy this week helping dad to get ready for the frantic fish-ing opener."

Chad walked further away, and yelled back that he will bring some interesting videos and a plastic gro-cery bag full of various newspaper articles when he returned in a couple days, so I can be brought up to date.

Chad went on to say, "Remember I soon graduate

and we will be busting ass together here this summer remodeling and insulating another cabin for snowmobilers, since there is an excellent trail system close by."

We anticipate that the FBI will be finally releasing some information on why they've got their man, and how they have promised but have not delivered on that scenario for a good couple of weeks.

Chad told me some disparaging news when he said, "Tom, I will bolster your spirits with these parting thoughts: this nation and more and more citizens and world to some degree, we hope and pray, are now starting to notice a faint odor."

I responded, "Thanks, Chad," as I probably stupidly think to myself about a competitor high school team that year's back had the sports name *Spoilers*. I also believe I have some long overdue praying to catch up on.

Chad went on to say, "Well Tommy, I'm sure no one will notice us carrying on this almost long distance conversation but I have places to go and things to do."

We both raise our fists and yell for the team! I have mixed feelings as I see Chad drive off. I read my instructions for which cabin I'm working on this week and take a quick couple hour nap before venturing forth to practically give my car away.

The days just seem to roll by while kind of melding together. It's a good thing I'm performing some menial bull, tear-up work, because my mind is in full overload mode and the physical stuff helps relax me. I'm very anxious to see and hear from Chad. This afternoon was very upsetting to me when a fisherman in a party of three seems really perplexed about where he has seen me before.

I'm taking the Liberty of some info between chapters-- **Anti-terror law may spawn huge intelligence apparatus**

By Jim McGee, Washington Post last update November 03, 2001-11.00 PM

Washington D.C.—Molded by wartime politics and passed a week and a half ago with furious speed, the new anti-terrorism bill lays the foundation for a domestic intelligence gathering system of unprecedented scale.

Overshadowed by the public focus on new internet surveillance and "roving wiretaps" were numerous features that will enable the Bush administration to make fundamental changes at the FBI, the CIA and the Treasury Department.

Known as the U.S.A. Patriot Act, the law empowers the government to shift the primary mission of the FBI from solving crimes to gathering domestic intelligence. In addition, the Treasury has been charged with building a financial intelligence-gathering system whose data can be accessed by the CIA.

Most significantly, the CIA will have the authority for

the first time to influence FBI surveillance operations inside the United States and to obtain evidence gathered by Federal grand juries and criminal wiretaps. The law reflects how profoundly the attacks changed the nation's thinking about the balance between domestic security and civil rights. (For brevity I stopped at this juncture of the article but for more have at it)

C.A.

I Carl Aabye, believe Military Combatant Status was initiated during W.W

Two because of (Real or imagined fear of infiltrators or domestic sympathizers

with dubious intentions) C.A.

I am inserting some excerpts from Nat Henhoff a nationally renowned authority on the First amendment and the Bill of Rights and the author of many books.

His column is distributed by United Media

Stuart Taylor- in the Dec. 18 widely respected National Journal- added that while he doesn't doubt that there are close calls in some of these hearings, "the current process is so flawed as to allow for indefinite detention even of detainees who could produce conclusive proof, if given fair hearings, that they have nothing to do with terrorists. Congress needs to fix this."

Congress needs to fix a lot more- including the National Security Agency's lawless, **warrantless spying on Americans** and the CIA's "renditions" of suspects to be tortured in other countries- special CIA powers

and authorized by the President, although Outside all
American and International laws.

Chapter Three --------- NEW DEVELOPMENTS

I think I could be getting depressed, and although I hadn't really busted ass today I felt exhausted, and I decided to go to bed early. I wake up yelling and feel disoriented when I finally realized that Chad is shaking me awake. We apologize, and then we both start laughing and between the two of us we can't stop. Chad has valuable information for me and said, "Tommy, do you want the good news first or the bad." We both looked at one another completely dumbfounded. Moreover, being young and dumb, we repeated the laughing thing. I conclude that Chad is drunk or worse. It eventually comes to me; he is emotionally drained and seriously sleep deprived.

Chad exclaimed:

Tom-Ass you dumb ass, I drove well over a thousand miles on this crap and those timed gory-ass pictures. I do believe though that your graphic digital pictures were the hooks. Tom, some new level-the-playing-field heavy weights I contacted for our team said thanks a lot, in the most sarcastic of ways and can you believe I also had luck in establishing communication with your family members?

I replied, God Chad, thank you, thank you!"

Chad reciprocated and said,

Tommy, your voice surely has a completely different

ring to it than your new brain trust uttered, and Linda
said not to worry and pity the poor souls that have
illegally parked Dad and his and our new power of
the pen. She said she would gladly fill in as Daddy for
you with Julie, until your triumphant return. Oh shit,
Carl, I'm sorry, I wasn't thinking. I thought you knew!
I feel so stupid that I even went and called you by your
real name again. You look like a deer caught in head-
lights but this is important, regardless of her condition
don't, I repeat don't even think of trying to freelance
or contact Julie on your own.

I feel light headed and said, "Chad what's the tripod
and camera doing in my cabin?"

"Well Tom, that's the law Professor's excess hardware
and he wants you to read this and sign it, if you so
agree."

I read the short note that wants my recall of events
roughly six hours before, during and after the event.
I'm requested to give permission on film for content,
and the possibility of excerpts to be used by my team,
and that this is a truthful and freely given telling of
events in my own words. I also read that my signing
in effect makes this a work product between me, and
my now by signing, official mouthpiece, Professor of
Law-- Vernon Vox.

"Well Chad, give me the other good, bad and the ugly,
from my sister Linda and company back home."

"Tom I'm ahead of you. After I left the big city and
was driving in the backcountry and within an hour of

here, I took the liberty to pull off the road to practice my acting and taped all I could recall. Besides, that way you can listen in privacy, as I can't take watching a grown man cry."

I questioned Chad again, "Chad, what the hell time is it?"

"Ten thirty P.M. so you missed the local television news."

I responded, "Oh boy, I thought it was at least five in the morning. Well, I won't be able to sleep now so make sure I can watch your cameo appearance and then get the hell out of here, as some old movie starlet supposedly said, 'I vaunt to be alone."

"You got that right there Thomas, and I almost forgot something important, our teams password is get this: Ufta Frieda and something that sounds like a baby deer or fawn and don't ask me to spell it. Don't look at me it's our Norwegian- University Of Minnesota Law Professor's creation. Goodnight Tom, see you in the morning."

Chapter Four ------------ Time in a Rowboat

The following morning Chad pries me out of bed, and
after a rough awakening I start to feel pretty good.
Moreover, I was up half the night performing my video, and I was listening and re-listening to Linda's
voice that Chad conveniently forgot to inform me was
also on his tape.
Chad explained, "Tom, I'll take your video and
quickly get it off to our anxious mad Professor."
The next few days fly by as Chad and I talked, while
working on some cabins. Chad and his folks will be
traveling to our university at Grand Forks, North Dakota this weekend for Chad's graduation. Chad will be
receiving his law Degree or whatever. I'm both nervous and excited at the thought of running this place
all by myself. Graduation day is here and they are
about to leave. I hear them laugh as they inform me I
will have an experienced helper showing up. Sure
enough an hour later Phyllis shows up, although she
must be more than twenty years my senior she sure is
shapely and attractive. Just having her around certainly helps; she's a workhorse. I try to control my un-
due attention towards her, although if her backside is
toward me my glances may linger. We got along and
had fun dividing up our duties. Gee, I now feel a little
guilty and somewhat down as I think about the fact

I'm going to be a Dad. A few days go by faster than I thought they would. . It's Sunday morning already. I decided to rake up the beach area again when a tall, rangy, fifty-to-sixty year old man with a golf type hat walks up to me with his fishing gear, and he leans toward me and says, "Ufta Frieda Faun. It's great to be alive on such a glorious day." He informs me that he is paying my wages and there is a bonus for me to assist him. Moreover, I was to be his personal guide in a fishing endeavor. He quickly locates an old out-of-service cedar strip rowboat, and he tells me that I may have to bail some water today until she swells some. We dragged the boat to the lake and slide her in. Not seeing a virtual flood of water; we loaded up and we put our Mae West life jackets on. He looks the oars and oar locks over, and he then throws the oldest small outboard I've ever seen in the boat for good measure. We push off for open water, and I start rowing and watching for incoming water.

I greeted Professor Vox and said, "Mr. Vern Vox I presume!"

Professor Vox responded,

"Tommy, I was captivated by your story and your digital image, but it's Vernon Vox to you and anyone who appreciates the value of my total life experience."

I explained to the professor and said, "Well, professor, as long as I already started out on the wrong foot, I've thought about your last name sounding Duchy, I believe I have seen a Holland produced vodka by that handle."

The professor professed to me,

"Tommy, I'm quite sure my family's last name was longer over in Norway before they emigrated around 1850 by coming thru Southeastern Canada and eventually Quebec. Moreover, they came by boat down the Great Lakes to Wisconsin, and then they finally landed in Southeastern Minnesota. Although you may be on to something as there is a good chance that several mere thousand years back sometime after the last Ice Age that Germanic tribes that lived along the North Sea were proficient in boat transportation. You see they shoved off from the present day Netherlands area for the now melted Northlands of Scandinavia. Moreover, upon their arrival the aggressive ones pushed people who got there before them possibly from Central Asia, to the north.

I questioned the Vox, "Professor, were those reindeer herders the Saami or Laplanders?"

The professor was amazed to find that I was interested in this history when he said, "Very good, Tommy, only they didn't start with the reindeer until the Norse showed them how in the Eighteenth Century. Now where are all the sunfish?"

I answered, "Oh, way over to a bay on the far east end."

The professor continued on:

Well, Tommy, let me row, and I'll tell you some more

little talked about knowledge of the Vikings' Eastern route travels. Tom our relatives: the Vikings had their day for a couple hundred years and they were not so romantic at the time when they traded with the strong and plundered the weak as they traveled the known world and more. Their boats were unique in that they could travel the seas as well as capable of navigating in shallow waters and rivers. They roamed far inland on rivers that emptied to the seas. The rivers to the Baltic Sea were avenues they traveled far inland to as close to the source as they could. At these far interior places in Russia they commandeered the local people that they called their slaves, hence becoming known as Slavic people to portage their boats and goods to new rivers that emptied into the Black Sea or the Mediterranean Sea. Moreover, they visited Italy and Greece, and they even introduced The Greek Orthodox Religion to the Slavic people on their return trips back home. The Slavs always had a hard time managing the many diverse regions, cultures, and people. The two invited powerful Rusvik brothers from Scandinavia or more specifically present day Sweden came to run things, hence the name for the area became known as Russia. I know most people are also aware of our relatives' ventures into Ireland, especially the Belfast area with its' many people staying until they eventually assimilated into the population, while some others even took Irish wives on to Iceland. Did you also know that the Christopher Columbus family shield showed his

family resided in Norway 400 years previous to his
trips to the Caribbean area? There is speculation that
he had in his possession an old Nordic map or two.
Columbus and many others knew the world was
round, but they thought it was only half as big as it is.
Moreover, they would have run out of provisions if the
new world wasn't in his way to getting to India, al-
though he thought he found it and the Indians of India
to his dying day. Hell, Tommy, even Leif Erickson's
brother Thorvald proclaimed in Vineland (present day
Maine 1,000 years ago) with a fatal arrow wound to
the midsection. There is fat around me belly and this
is a luscious, wonderful land we discovered, but too
bad I won't be around to enjoy it.

We make it to our fishing spot, and the professor is
relatively quiet. I think to myself if he knows as much
about our Federal Justice System as Nordic history
hopefully things will become interesting. I could see
that he now appears to be doing some serous thinking.

The professor continues conversation,
Tom, you're lucky that you have Chad for your friend
and vise versa. We need to get the pendulum coming
back to the center, and we will work for our breaks,
but a little luck wouldn't hurt. We will cast our nets
far, wide and deep. I will be the visible point man and
lightning rod moreover I have to admit to being a little
excited at my late stage of life in getting a chance to
put Humpty Dumpy back together again.

Vernon puts his old antique outboard on the boats

transom, and then he puts his large hands on each side of the smooth aluminum flywheel, and he gives a few spins and it fires up. We aren't doing much over trolling speed, so I cast my bait toward our direction of travel and retrieve a few times.

I notice Professor Vox is watching me and he says, *I see you're a lefty, but that's not surprising. Tommy you know the term that timing is everything? It just hit me that it didn't take long for the Patriot Act to be passed by Congress and signed into law with only a lone Senator from Wisconsin not having his vision clouded. Tommy Carl how about that name? The other thing that many- many page document didn't just instantly appear, it had been on a shelf somewhere!* Upon getting back we unload and I help him load his old station wagon.

The professor shares his feelings, *Tom I needed to see you in the flesh to look you in the eye, and I regret we have to now avoid each other like the Bubonic or Black Plague that devastated Norway, Europe, and the World. This is huge, and in the words of two past black leaders keeps the faith baby; we shall overcome. Oh Tom, I also couldn't find any instances of the F.B.I. checking out you or your Dad's local library reading habits, but then the law prevents library personnel from publicly reporting such activity. I do sense people at the grass roots level are becoming alarmed about the erosion of our Bill of Rights, our Constitution, and the government's sneak*

*and peek- unannounced actions. Moreover, search
warrants based on any sniff from any source that
brings up foreign intelligence against anything domestic in our country. Well, I feel chilled even if it isn't
cold, but I will; I promise you, warm up to the task
ahead of us all.*

I help Vernon fuel up for his trip back home and he
hands me a sealed envelope, which informs me on the
outside that is from one of his independent confidants.

I then decided to share a story too,

*Professor you are a great story teller but my gramps
told me why the Norwegians decided because of raw
numbers to go the route of passive resistance in World
War Two. Upon taking over a large building in Oslo
for an administrative headquarters the Germans decided to keep a Norwegian clerk who can speak Ger-
man and knows the building and all its contents. His
desk sat in front of a large wall mural of many years
back Viking long boats out to sea. One day a high-
ranking officer clicks his heels and approaches the
clerk's desk with his arm and a finger pointing at the
many ships. He forcefully asks "vat's dat, vor ships?"
The clerk casually turned and looked at the ships and
then looks the officer in the eye and replies, yes that
represents our two hundred year occupations and in-
tervention of the British Isle, by the way how are you
folks coming in England?*

The stoic Vox makes a sneezing thru his nose sound,
and he is choking and laughing as he climbs in his car

to depart and I hear him saying over and over vats that Vor Ships Vor Ships. I decided before I retired to bed for the evening to pull the envelope out and read with interest. You can call me Mr. T. for trouble or Mr. U. for you. It said he watched my video with interest. He goes on to say that he has through the years gained Mr. Vox's confidence to make independent decisions. I don't tell, and he doesn't want to know about my devious ways. P.S. Request for your billfold minus credit cards and valued photos etc., but leave intact your driver's license and any miscellaneous items. I marvel at his planned method of transit or shipment, but I need to quit speculating, and I have to try to get some sleep. I'm not good at even taking orders from myself, and I start conniving; no planning how to make contact and see the mother of our future child to be.

Chapter Five ------------------ Ill Advised Trip?

This morning after coffee, eggs and toast, I decided to ask a favor. "Phyllis, could you give me a ride to where I sold my old car. I want to scrounge through some used junk, and I can find my own way back as it's an easy walk of less than ten miles?"

"Sure Tom, do you want to get there directly or take the longer scenic route."

"Just for today Philly I'd accept the less exciting short cut."

She got me there in one piece, and I crawled thru a barbwire fence. I started kicking things around as well as myself. The mean junkyard dog is now barking until he gets close enough to see I am not impressed, and he now remembers my scent and likeness. I'd previously played with him before when I sold my old wreck to his master. I am all wrapped up in petting and scratching the big baby when a hand on my shoulder and a voice startles me more than I want to let on.

Howe greets me and says, "Tom, you can knock on our door and we even have a door bell out here in the sticks or did you just want to scare the hell out of our scary watch dog?" We shake hands and he says, "What can I do for you today?"

"Howe, do you have any cheap wheels that might have a short trip or two left in her?"

"Well, Tommy me lad, I only guarantee until off me lot, but I'll sell you one for $50 and haul and buy back for $20."

"That's a deal Howy, if you fill it up with gas and let me work off the fuel bill."

I soon drive off with a full tank; I think he likes me. I now apprehensively but excitedly start out for my old hometown. Gosh I sort of wish he hadn't already pulled the motor from my car. Time and miles fly by as I brainstormed with myself on how to safely and with at least some degree of security make contact with Julie and company. It's aggravating when the best option seems to be to throw a rock and a note through her bedroom window. Maybe stupidly upon arriving back in my hometown I meander over to the closest thing our town has left of skid row. I visit with the patrons, and I pick a victim to telephone a message to Julie that alludes to a set time for a meeting where the two of us had first met. This cost me two bottles of beer, and I listened enough to make sure he was talking to her.

I start out for our largest shopping center and the orange juice based specialty shop. I see she beat me here, and I try to restrain my emotions from completely taking over. We both just sit looking and absorbing each other for a long couple minutes. It seems hard for either of us to say anything, and what to say first.

Then thank God she says, "Glad to see you. You look

okay! I am hanging in there the best I can."

"Julie, I don't know where to start, but keep the faith."

I know tears are coming down my cheeks. "Julie, I
picked you as our designated driver that night for a
reason, and if you will have me; I want you and our
family to be designated partners for life."

We settled down had a nice; no a great time. We made
attempts for our hard departure as I hand her a large
envelope of information that I had put together at a
small shopping center in a little town on my way here.
I provide a copy of my cameo video that professor
Vox requested and stressed the importance of complete confidentiality.

Julie continued on to say, "Carl, I have a safe neutral
place to store this, after I study the hell out of it."

One final embrace, and in a daze I reluctantly head
north again. I feel a good emotionally drained if that
makes any sense. Actually I drive east first, and at the
second town I must have come back down to earth
enough to feel some hunger pangs. I pull in at a con-
venience store where I know they have various hot
dogs etc, and I load up with, as much garnishment as I
think is humanly possible.

In a triumphant mood; I pull out on the major state
highway.

I thought to myself, "My God, no steering!" I can turn
the steering wheel but nothing happens. I let up on the
gas, and I am so far one lucky son-of-a-bitch with
there being a driveway directly across from me, but

now oncoming traffic is hurtling toward me with horns blaring. I frantically wave at them, and I try to judge their ability to stop as their tires are now squealing from heavy braking, and I try to keep my eyes open while trying to judge the maximum that I can accelerate so that I would be able to still stop before I plow head on into parked cars located in a used car lot just ahead of me at the leading edge of a frontage road. Whew! I hope that wasn't as close as I thought it was. I hope no one calls law enforcement. I jumped out and kicked the tires to see if they will move. Moreover, my luck is still holding to some small degree. I find a bumper jack, and a well hidden fifth of Gramps old favorite booze, Ancient Age. I use a small pothole to jack from to get my tires in a direction that has possibilities of getting me on the property of a nearby repair shop. I limp it over, and I finagled an older mechanic to jack it up so that we can look it over. He half jokingly asks me if I have any enemies; the car looks like it had sat in high grass or it had been in a wet spot that dried out now and then. A local town cop slowly drives by, and we both wave to him. The old gent asks me my plans for this automotive refugee from hell. I tell him it is going directly to a salvage yard near where I work.

"Alright Son, but in all my years I've never seen this happen to a steering sector before! Young man, didn't the steering get a little wild after it swung down on the frame before the thing completely separated?"

I responded,

Yeah it steered like an old International corn binder:
the kind that you just steer the opposite of your travel
to stay ahead of the game, but while the steering on
this thing wasn't anything to write home about this old
pot-holed, heavy-traveled highway, if you ask me,
needs another complete overlay of asphalt.

I ask the station attendant, "Sir, do you have a
rest room I could use?"

He answered, "You bet, it's around the back side of
the building and I can see where you would need to
check your shorts."

He is laughing so hard his face is red and snot is running out his nose, but I love him anyway as he attempts to tell me how he could but wouldn't
recommend half ass repairing this clunker,

"Son, I'll tell you what an idiot might do to nurse it
home and get it the hell off the roads."

It wasn't long before I was digging through some
bolts in a big old wash pan and he ignored me as I
soon had my steering sector back in place and reat-
tached and I slowly drive off. I take back roads and
pure will it back to the bone yard. Howe comes out
and we negotiate the car for my gas bill and a ride
back to the resort. I'm back at my cabin for only a
short time when Jim, Stella and Chad come rolling in.

I walk over and congratulate the new Law School
grad.

Chad asked, "Tom, how's it been going?"

I respond, "Oh, it's been going Mr. Barrister."

Chad went on to say, "Well Tom, I can't practice before the Bar as of yet and we're not in England either. Well, I'm going to retire; it's been a hectic schedule the last few days."

I reciprocated, "Good idea, Chad but just think in Austria you would be a Master of Law."

The next days we worked on remodeling cabins, and Chad informs me he is going to the Fargo-Moorhead area on business: his, mine, and ours and he wanted to know if there is anything I miss or want from my past life.

I exclaimed, " Chad, I know you are not a gamer, but I felt a couple of man on the run type games have served me to a degree, but now I no longer have postpartum for my MP3 player."

Upon his return in a day and a half he had a serious look on his face. Chad informed me when he said:

Tom, your sister Linda tells me the F.B.I. served a search warrant at your girlfriend Julie's residence. The F.B.I., we also speculate, can't hold your Dad indefinitely and the public relations campaign is important and working. Also, get this: the promised news conference, they keep moving back, is almost upon us, but I have been advised to not go because there will be eyes checking on interested parties. Now do you want the good news?

I replied, "Just let me have it."

Chad continued to say:

We will have ringers or correspondents at the event with leading questions and as they avoid one, we will pepper them again and hope it gets contagious. We hope to get them or him or her, locked in on some issues. By the way, I almost forgot that in today's newspaper you are reported missing, after renting a small boat off the east coast of Mexico and presumed drowned, as only the overturned small boat is recovered.

I replied, "God Chad, I wonder if Dad will be informed, and what effect that could have on any possible interrogation he is undergoing."

Chad continued:

Who knows Tom, the road to hell is filled with many a good intention. I speculate that on that fateful day your Dad entered the back door, spotted his out of place AK-47 and overheard an agent talking on the phone to headquarters. We were also able to verify a 911-cell call, from your Dad's analog phone that day at 10:13 A.M. The emergency phone people were also flat out informed not to release the recorded 9-1-1 phone content until and unless court ordered.

I filled Chad in with the details of my educated speculation, "Chad, I just know the old man upon spotting his rifle and sensing the men in the dinning room would call 911 from the kitchen area and calmly put his cell phone in his shirt pocket while swinging his AK-47 into the next room as he was barking out his location, name and conditions."

Chad shook his head and thought, "That could well be. By reports from neighbors men in suits, and the local police with their sirens blasting had converged that day at almost the same time.

I replied," It's about time for the nighttime news and I need some help with a crossword puzzle so Chad come on with me to my cabin for a while."

The television news comes on and nothing shows up until it is almost time for the weather. There it is; a casual mention of the now new set time of 11:30 A.M this Friday, for a news conference explaining the National Security necessity of continuing to hold a local man: Carl Hanson as a military combatant until more investigative material is analyzed or a petition for his release from such status is formalized with the Justice Department.

Chad wondered, "Tom, I wonder if they have transported your Dad out of the Country.

I wondered, "Chad, why in the hell would they do that."

Chad responded, "Tommy disregard or strike my last statement, and you and I now have a standing appointment to view this event on a large screen television that is closer to the broadcast station."

Chapter Six---------Interesting Event

Friday morning is finally here and we took a day off from work and drive almost 40 miles to a quaint resort with a dining room/dance hall where the television reception is better. Of course we wouldn't miss this event no matter how it might go. Chad and I both ordered burger baskets and beer. We sat with our pens and papers as we waited with anticipation to score the main event. I remembered, "Chad this brings back memories to me of the F.B.I. releasing information to a demanding public of an airline flight that mysteriously crashed in the summer of the mid nineties, shortly after take off from New York to France." Finally, the time is here, as the station breaks away for coverage of this event.

Jeff Harris introduces himself, and he says,

Let us introduce ourselves today to a good showing of the news media and interested citizens. For those that don't know me, my name is Jeff Harris, a 30-year veteran of the F.B.I., stationed in the regional office here in Fargo, North Dakota. I now give you Agent Alice Hanson.

Alice Hanson introduces herself, and she says,

Thank you Jeff, I am Alice Hanson, I believe not a relative to a party that brings us together here today. I have held an Administrative Post in our Minneapolis division for the last five years of my almost 20 years of

service. I hope to answer any questions any of you

may have, but first I again give you Jeff so he can lay

out why we need all the tools we have at our disposal

to win this war on terrorism.

Harris continues, "First of all I want to stress the Patriot Act of 2001 it has not been shown to erode to any degree our basic American rights. Also of importance, if such was shown to occur, Congress has the power and duty to change or repeal the laws of our land.

With that said we are open for a few questions."

Harris is quested, "Mr. Harris, does the Lone Wolf provision of 1978 come into play here, or help as yet another tool?"

Harris answers, "I do believe this group has done their homework, and yes and yes as it removes our burden of having to show a direct connection to subversive organizations or groups. "Alright you young lady."

Young lady continues,

People are wondering if the poor agents were let in or

knocked down and rushed in with a search warrant.

Moreover, some people asked me if it was one of those

new Warrant to come Later, sneak and peek opera-

tions derived from the Patriot Act. In addition, some

rumors are going around that you even had a warrant

or judge or court O.K. to have placed some kind of

G.P.S. thing on Mr. Hanson's car.

Harris continues, "That's certainly a lot of information, but we don't divulge our investigative methods, while we are aware of some of your terminology we don't call it that. We need to do our job under trying circumstances to protect our citizens. O.K. you back there."

Concerned citizen questions Harris, "Does your branch have a code of revenge to avenge fellow agents if the law is lacking?"

Harris responds, "Hum, Um, do you want that one Alice?"

Hanson answers,

I admit we are amazed by some of the questions we get, and we usually don't answer a hypothetical, but today I will throw one back at you. First of all, we don't condone vigilante justice, but do you think groups of people say, Doctors, have ever between themselves had a pact on end of life issues, on a personal level? Again, I want to emphasize the bureau would come down with full force, if there was even a whisper of such. O.K., you over there, with the plaid shirt.

Person in Plaid shirt asked, "What about habeas corpus, due process and the right to answer charges, and is it true Mr. Hanson made a 911 call from his home at the approximate time of the agents demise and that some of their issued inventory is missing?"

Hanson replies, "Those are of an investigative nature as Agent Harris stressed so I couldn't answer that if I knew. Also, I am sorry that I don't recognize you, could you give your name and the organization you represent here today."

Smith replies, "I am Paul Smith of your sister city and with the Pioneer Press."

Hanson ends the press conference:

Thank you, and that is all for today, but I am personally surprised that with all the public relation onslaught that someone is lacking, or ignoring Carl's possible release, by not even filing with the court a simple petition for his release from custody or a request to be timely charged with a crime and again thank you Agent Harris and everyone here today for their hospitality.

Now a young female reporter is yelling and pleading for one last question. She is determined and persistent as she somehow closes in on the agents.

I question, "Chad don't you think Agent Jeff Harris looks perplexed as the television cameras continue rolling. Look at that, Chad; he is going to take her question."

Young lady questions Harris, "Sir, were there thumb prints on the weapon from a right or left-handed shooter, and was there gunpowder residue on the alleged Mr. Carl Hanson, Senior?"

Harris responds, "Well, young lady, I assume you are a viewer of television forensic shows and be assured we follow all proper protocol in our investigations.

Again thank you all today."

I question Chad, and I said, "What do you think Chad; did they have the body language of wanting to get the hell out of there?"

Chad answers: and he said:

You better believe it baby, although Agent Hanson was a lot cooler than her red-faced partner for today. Tom if I may editorialize, A.W.O.L. big time for Congress yet again, because if President George W. Bush can be accused of abuse of power, then Congress should be vilified for being derelict in duty. I don't know about you but I'm more pissed than ever over the fact that this so called Patriot Act is the most rushed and flawed legislation since the Alien and Sedition Act!

We had a few more beers and engage in small talk. I think to myself; you're pissed off. Then we finally start on our meandering trip back home.

Chad's conjecture during drive back:

Tom, I really believe they are hoping to find a way to dispense of your Dad's military combatant status and there must be internal conflict within the bureau that we couldn't begin to understand, and can you imagine their worst nightmares coming true by some of the rumor and specifics that shook loose today. Also, before I forget, something today made me decide to give you one of my unused debit cards and pin number in the event of an emergency. Another thing if events warrant I know you have mastered how to start and run our old garbage detail pickup.

I replied, "Chad, I see you were glancing at what I wrote down today, so here it is a full confession of a trip I made to Fargo-Moorhead when you and your parent's were up at Grand Forks for your graduation. I don't want to even attempt to articulate my confusion and concerns of the search warrant at Julie's." Chad continues, and he said, "I'm with you on that, and I hope there wasn't any connection to your unscheduled trip back home. I also forgot to pass on to you some hearsay that someone in your Dad's neighborhood, that fateful morning, saw five men sitting in a car three quarters of a block away and after almost an hour, three from the back seat got out and walked toward your house."

The next week flies by with a high turnover of campers and fishermen. Every couple days, Chad drives off for phone calls with someone, but he won't tell me anything directly. One rather distinguished looking guest at our resort who refers to himself as Andrew caught my eye or I caught his. I can't decide if he is an old looking fifty or a young looking seventy. I now somehow sense something, and I look over and a bit behind me and this fellow Andrew is just studying and staring at me. He starts smiling and waving at me like we are long lost friends.

A little after supper Chad came over to my cabin, and he informs me that Andrew is a lonesome, but very financially comfortable- widowed- retired salesman. He would value our company this evening for a few hours of companionship, fishing, and imported beer.

"Chad, do you know this guy from past seasons?"

Chad answered, "I only know he will dribble some

good bucks for our professional guide and bullshit session."

I ended the conversation and said, "Sorry to defer Chad but I am going to hit the sack early as I am getting one hell of a migraine headache."

I waited and watched as they finally push off shore for the open lake. I guess my dam paranoia is taking over again, and I use my passkey to enter this Andrew fellow's cabin. Apparently a small piece of paper had been placed somewhere in the door and is now fluttering to the floor. Well, what the hell, I am already in so I better check for that rat I thought I saw earlier today looking out at me through one of Andrew's particular cabin windows. Everything seems to be of the normal variety then I even check out the little freezer in this old refrigerator. Dam, a pistol wrapped in some freezer paper; in a near panic its like ground zero again. Be still my racing heart I keep telling myself as I dam near puke. My mind is racing; maybe I am overthinking, but I just can't take more of this self-imposed fugitive status.

My mind is in such overload that I next find myself sitting on the edge of my cabins bed and I reach underneath and crack open the over thirty year old dusty fifth of Ancient Age. (How fitting) I had a couple cans of Coke for mix in my fridge. I'm sampling and thinking this stuff doesn't have much of a kick to it. I must have been sitting here resting my eyes for a time when Chad dam near bumped me off my bed. "Here

Chadwick, chugalug some of this antiquity."

"Tom get your ass off the pity pot because were at a critical Juncture."

"Fuck you Chadwick: your intersections and the rest of your Yale buddy bone heads. You God Dam Lawyers sure have us all in a World of shit." **Whack**;" by God Chadwick try that one again." I felt tingling all thru my extremities on that sucker. I hope I bluffed him into not slapping me again as I still see stars. Chad still looks agitated, "Now listen closely Mr. Hanson, we must be doing something because a Maryland smut-writer featured mid life crisis, American men with too much money, time and Viagra, vacationing in Southeast Asia. I just checked my mail from a Mr. T today. Here does that possibly look like your Dad shaking hands with a real young female in a foreign land."

"Oh shit Chad how bad could something like this be!"

"Carl, it could actually be a good sign when they feel they need to reach in that **bag** and by not coming fishing with us tonight you may have perked this Andy fellow's curiosity."

I put on that I was about to pass out but I am now pretty Dam sober and Chad finally leaves. My fears are heightened further of putting Chad and his parents or anyone near me in jeopardy. I start writing Chad a letter telling him I'm leaving and why. I relay that I will attempt to call him at 8 P.M. every Friday night at the nearby Lunker Lodge and to please give a sealed

letter to Julie if I become predisposed to do so personally. I also plan for a final showdown to resolve this
thing one way or another! Then a postscript: keep a
good balance in your debit card account, and if I can't
personally repay you someday, I would put money on
it that you or my Dad will recoup from writing your
book.

Chapter Seven—Interlude with Jeff Harris F.B.I.
and his wife Betty

Betty asked, "Jeffrey, you've hardly touched your supper, what's bothering you?"

Harris answered, "Betty, I want to talk about it but I can't."

"Jeffrey it's that Hanson matter isn't it?" I watched the news conference and I know something isn't right."

Agent Jeff Harris replied:

Betty, someone is holding bigger and more cards than we realized and they could have by now gotten his status changed, but now public opinion, cover-up fever and other things are building and I am deeply worried. I personally think we should have released Hanson from that horse shit military combatant status long ago, but the powers that be in the Bureau or elsewhere must feel that would be admitting wrongdoing on our part.

"Jeff I know you feel your Agency gets too big for their britches now and again."

"Sweetheart did I ever say that; but I have heard rumblings from the Civil Liberties Union, and if some key members of Congress ever push for congressional hearings- well policy and heads will roll on this one!"

"Jeffrey darling you need to get your blood pressure

checked again as during your television appearance your face was nearly as red as it was tonight before supper when you said you had just come from that urgent meeting with your supervisors."

Chapter Eight ---------Heading for a Standoff

Three A.M. and I'm out of here in the Teigan's old Chevy half ton, and I don't want to look back. I love the people and place. I drive along and as usual my mind is moving faster than this old trusty pickup. Maybe I could resolve this quicker if I picked a more local town, like our Climax, Minnesota. Too bad the Belmont Giant isn't still around that area for me to befriend. Oh yes, the Giant who was born in Anthony, Iowa of Norwegian descent in the 1800s. Moreover, him, his parents, and brothers had moved to Belmont Township in North Dakota on the west bank of the Red River across from Minnesota where the Sand Hill River empties. I read that his father was only a little over six-foot, and two hundred pounds, but the boys were all three and four hundred pounds of humanity until the big brother came along. The big boy built his own customized furniture, and he won $100.00 by carrying a plow across the nearby town of Climax Minnesota at fair time. That would be well over a Grand in today's money for the large boned and mus-cled man the kids of that day all loved. I someday hope to locate his gravesite. He was buried in a piano case, and I believe a pair of his pants is in a museum in Hillsboro, North Dakota. How and why that town wrested the county seat from Caledonia is an interest-ing rest of the story in itself. I admit to some second thoughts, but drive ahead. I drove west on the gently winding scenic State Highway 113. It reminded me in a way of traveling down a beautiful meandering river with a fresh view of sights around every bend. I swear I just drove by a lake with a stunning view of an island that Gramps had on a Hamm's beer poster from years back. I make a decision to stop by the game refuge where I hid the digital camera of one of the men I shot. I quickly recover from a hollow spot in an old tree. It looks to have withstood time and the elements. I am so charged up that as I was driving through the Twin Cities at near midnight I decide to just drive on as long as I am able to continue. Around 1:00 A.M. I must have been running out of adrenaline, and I decided to pull over at a rest stop near Northfield, Minnesota. I slept until 6 A.M, and upon getting the cobwebs out Think no way will I make a final stand here as I'm not yet fully armed, and I remember reading this had been a bad spot for Jesse James and the boys. I drove a ways to the small town of Kenyon. I always planned to check out a museum there, and this is the town where a nearby church called Holden is located. Holden is where our relatives had first settled after leaving Norway in 1852. They had also as professor Vox's relatives, traversed the cheaper route by way of Quebec. Next, they transported by boat down the Great Lakes, then rail boxcar, and last by oxcart. I have read accounts that Oline: wife of my Great - Great Great Grandpa Tosten wrote that the cattle-car

ride on the rails was horrendous. I know Tostens' son
Andrew, Gr. Gr. Granddad and his young wife Inger
came up and started a general store twenty miles north
of Fargo Moorhead on the east bank of the Red River
of the North in 1880.

I finally have a feeling of satisfaction by finding their
parents Tosten and Oline's grave sites just west of the
Holden church, and I enjoy a relaxing and interesting
day, except for words from a dam song that I can't remember who sang it that keeps slamming around in
my head, -- *I'm going out in a blaze of glory.*

In the late after noon I made the decision to not travel
to Spirit Lake, Iowa where three of granddad's music
heroes played their last gig before their plane went
down in that ill-fated plane crash in February of 1959.
The bands were on the way ironically, to our town of
Moorhead, Minnesota. I also remember him telling me
that a guy by the name of Don some years later wrote
a long song commemorating that tragic event. Namely
The Day the Music Died or maybe it was called *American Pie.* I stopped in Decorah, Iowa for another first
on this mission, and I am on a mission. I know one of
Dad's great-grandfather's was raised in Forrest something Iowa; where he graduated from I believe a Lutheran seminary college near here. I also remember
seeing something in my travel near the Twin Cities of
a Bishop Whipple, who interceded with President
Abraham Lincoln to not hang another 250 more Indians than the 50 or so that already had there necks

stretched near present day Mankato, Minnesota for the uprising of 1862. I admit my thoughts are scrambled in my tired state. I also remember the tie-in that Dad's Great grandfather on his mother's side had; it was upon his graduating from college at Luther in the 1870s. He had also migrated up to the Red River pioneer town of Perley, Minnesota, and he was the young pastor of Kirkebo Lutheran Church. I was told that one day around 1890 he was 22 miles south in our present day town of Moorhead, and he discovered an Episcopal school named after Bishop Whipple. The church could be purchased for 10 grand, even though they had 30 grand into the land and buildings. My great-great-grandfather: J.M.O. as he was referred to or John Milton Orston Ness then diligently pursued funds in Crookston, East Grand Forks Minnesota, Grand Forks, North Dakota, and our Fargo-Moorhead area. I mean they wanted a Norwegian seminary school in the Red River Valley area, because after all the Swedes had Gustavas Adolphus. He must have been appreciated to some degree as there is a bronze relief of him behind Old Main, and he was President of newly started and renamed Concordia College Corporation for 37 years.

I continue onto the bigger city of Cedar Rapids, Iowa, and once again find a secluded spot to get some sleep in the cab of the pickup. I suppose this is foolhardy; I sure enough don't need to be hassled for my identification or driver's license. God that's right; some genius had talked me into surrendering mine. I had planned on getting some day work but this might now be a bitch. Morning again comes dam early, and I searched out a Norwegian blood transfusion: coffee. I believe a historical standoff destination is coming into focus between my subconscious and conscious mind. I will continue for now my Mother bird ritual of getting away from my nest or loved ones. I over hear a man talking in a restaurant, who reminds me of Dad because of his age and general appearance. I understand he is considering an overdue roofing job on a six-plex he owns. I picked up on the fact he has sticker shock from the bids he received. I am now a desperate but good salesman, and I give him a good price if he would assist me with the entire debris cleanup. I also made sure that the supplier of shingles would elevate all materials to the roof. We continue visiting and we hit it off well. He even tells me he will furnish me room and board in his six plex because he just happened to have an empty unit, which adjoins him and his wife's place. I followed him to his place, and I have him order a slide off truck dumpster for the tear off. He then contacts a young nephew for ground cleanup. I am anxious to begin the tear off as soon as some material, tools, and the crucial tarpaper gets here. He tells me he has an old garden tined spade, and I can start the tear off right away if I want. I told him no, I would wait for the tarpaper first as just as I always remember. If it should rain that water runs down hill.

The weather and my body are holding up pretty well. Some long intense working days tire me out, and it's now a fateful Friday evening. I had permission to use the owner's phone. I sat at a desk located in a den-like room. I was excited as well as apprehensive with pen and paper in hand. I am going to finally go for it. I was actually shaking when Chad finally got on the line, "Ufta Frieda their Chad, I think I am glad to get to talk to you."

Chad responds:

Tom hold onto to your shorts because things are starting to pop. An informant, who calls himself Deep Throat Two as from the Nixon-Watergate era, is now coming out of the woodwork. He claims through a newspaper correspondent, on the East Coast, to personally know someone whose life was saved in Viet Nam thanks to your Dad. Perhaps of more importance, it gives strong indications of him being a real recent retired, or still active, long time member of the F.B.I at a high level. They give a warning that pertinent and case specific information of an embarrassing nature will soon be forthcoming if they don't do the right thing and give Mr. Carl Hanson his day in court. He finished by saying he is well aware how difficult it is for an eagle letting go of its grip even if it's holding fool's gold and remember who knows, the shadow and Deep Throat Two know.

I respond, "Chad do you think this is legit or some

more dirty tricks from Mr. Trouble."

Chad answers "Tom I had entertained some of those same thoughts, but regardless your Dad just became a lot hotter potato. Are you okay physically and mentally?"

I continue, "Chad, I'm a lot better mentally after talking to you, and I feel something is coming into focus. Chad, I believe you can understand that this has to be resolved for Dad and me in some manner. I am a young man with, I hope to hell, future responsibilities, because I am a family man to be, know what I mean."

Chad continues, "Listen Tom, promise to keep a cool tool and to call me here at the same time this coming Tuesday evening, as something else of a promising and potentially interesting nature needs some closer scrutiny."

I agree, "Alright Chad, I hope to be done with this job by then and collect my grand plus, for some serious shopping."

I really bust ass for the next days. I finished and collected my grand plus in cash by noon on Monday. I next set my sights for a large well advertised gun show; this week in El Paso, Texas. I have worked and slept hard the last five days, and I will attempt to drive straight through. My God, as I drove along on these endless miles I say to myself, when they say things are bigger in Texas they sure as hell are right when it comes to distance. How about that; I just saw a road sign about Austin Texas and as Waylon sang it, Bob

Wills is still the king. I remember years back when a young friend helped convince us to switch gramps country music radio station and we found out in short order we didn't have much seniority. Then a couple years ago Dad had fun riding me about all the Willie, Waylon, and all the other Country music C.D.'s that I have. My mind keeps wandering. Thoughts of Julie race through my head. Julie has really been consuming my mind. I remember her when she was young or real young. The awkwardness of her teen years; the big crush she always had on me. She used to follow us guys everywhere we went or tried too. I feel bad; because I didn't understand how strong what I thought was just her puppy love was. Her dream will come true when I get out of this mess. We are going to be together. I have always wanted to get married, and have a family and have is now the key word. Julie I hope you can hang in there. I really do love her. Our situation has been driving me insane; I need to tell her of my hopes for the future. I will be graduating hopefully, if I can get out of this crap. I could buy her a ring. Feels like a dream, but I am going to make it come true. Ah, I just need to get through this mess! I cruise into El Paso in a daze, and finally find the large gun show here at this far western side of Texas. After visiting with some vendors I wondered how much trouble Dad in purchasing his assault weapons. I still have faith in my ability to finagle, talk, and press on. One fellow I met in the crowd bragged he was from the Crawford area, and he could get me whatever I wanted. I think that he picked up that I hadn't heard of this Crawford and he said, "Son you must not be a conservative then." I told him he was right, as I wanted to be real agreeable. He tells me it sounds to him like I need a Tech Nine, but they bring a premium price because of their ability to be concealed; due to their compact size. The price he quotes dam near knocks my socks off. I just started to walk away when an elderly African American gentleman lightly grabbed my shirt and discreetly follows me. We both finally sit down at a bench, and I see he is wearing a hearing aid. He tells me this latest model seems to do all right even with all this background noise.

The old gentleman said, "Young man for pure defensive purposes the most feared and reasonable; yet highly effective weapon is the sawed off 10 or 12 gauge shotgun."

He impresses me as being the equal of uncle Remus at spinning a yarn.

I follow him to his car, and we drove over to mine. From the trunk of his car he sells me an old double barrel; a box of proper shot; and a hacksaw with some high quality blades. He tells me a few tricks of the trade for preparing the up close and personal beast, but that all warranties are now off. Then as he enters his car to leave he waves and says, "bon voyage."

I caught him off guard when I blurted back, "Bon Jovi to you."

PASTOR
J.M.O. NESS
1851-1931

PHARMACIST
LARS CHRISTIANSON
1855-1946

FOUNDERS,

LEADERS,

BENEFACTORS

CONCORDIA CORPORATIO

PRESIDENT EARS   SECRETARY 43 YEARS

MEN OF VISION

Chapter Nine--------- One Hell of a Phone Call

I explore aimlessly around the immediate area, but I have one hell of a time locating a pay phone for our scheduled call, but sure as hell always keep my cell phone turned off, and the charged battery is in a separate location. I at least seemed to entertain one vendor when I purchased the largest size camouflage pants he carried and never expected to sell. I'm laughing; while he was folding them I was telling him they were for the Belmont Giant. I foolishly even feel a little cocky; as I finally made an expensive collect call for Chad back at the Lunker Resort Lounge. He is there, and he excitedly tells me of possible future considerations of Dad's status, in short, because of discovery or something to that effect his disposition is to be reviewed.

Chad explained:

Tom, dig this if you can, an invalid lady, not far from your Dad's neighborhood, has a serious hobby and equipment for receiving various, as in lots of, radio waves. She was apparently motivated by recent events to make one hell of a lot of copies, and generously distribute them to the media, and who knows where else. You were pretty prophetic. Just listen to my partial, but almost complete copy of your Dad's older style analog cell phone, but easier to intercept 911 call, that fateful day.

*Oh Tom, for more background, before I start the re-
cording, she heard your Dad's serious-sounding call
that day and started to record it. Your Dad, thank
goodness, apparently repeated his name and location
several times that morning.*

In the distance I hear inaudible muffled sound. Then
loud and clear I can hear Dad's booming voice, and I
lose it. I think I hear Chad sniffing too.

In about twenty seconds I compose myself, "Chad,
please start again from the beginning."

Chad gives me the run:

*Hanson at 906 13ᵗʰ Street South, Moorhead, there are
three badly shot up dead looking men on my living
room floor, and there will be two more just like them,
if these two who must have shot them make the slight-
est flinch. All right, you two, you got one chance to get
this right. Raise both your hands while slowly turning
your backside to me. Good now mosey side by side.
Good now slowly drop to your knees. Mighty fine, now
keep those hands up and belly flop to the floor. Real
nice and keep your fingers spread.*

*O.K. nine- one- one-people you still with me? Great,
now sound those sirens. I just returned home and got
the drop on these guys, one was on his cell phone and
the other was on his hands and knees on my living
room floor with the blood and guts as if trying to offer
first aid. This is important, sound your sirens so I
know you are on the way or I may feel these two will
make a threatening move and I will be forced to de-*

fend my self in my own castle. What did you just insin-
uate: Damn it I sure as hell didn't let them in, and one
more smart ass remark like that and I'll shoot these
son's a bitches too!"

I am so proud as I hear Dad keep repeating himself
until I can now hear the police sirens over his phone in
the distance. I bet they sounded sweeter to Dad at the
time than they had to me that day. I'm amazed at the
bonus of hearing new voices take some control of the
situation and I believe I hear someone say, "Alright
you can assume temporary custody of Mr. Hanson, but
he will shortly be under Federal Jurisdiction." A little
more indistinguishable gibberish and Dad's phone
went dead.

I exclaimed, "Chad, thank you for being you, but
these sands of Texas, El Paso have me exhausted."
Chad reciprocates, "Now Tom, don't panic or over
react again."

I continue to over react:

Dam it Chad I am actually not a person that is prone
to be a reactionary type. I have decided though to
make my final stand where in a way frontier justice
actually came to an end, and the standard criminal
justice system filled the void. Chad, do you all want to
mosey down at high noon this Friday for another ass
kicking, shootout, at the O.K. Corral, at Tombstone
Arizona?

Chad answers, "Tom, get serous do we want to, you
can bet your sweet ass on that! We will probably dou-

ble the couple thousand population of that little former silver mining town. Call me on my cell phone at 11:00 A.M. this Friday morning for a media escort, and I actually like the timing, place, idea, and we will as in we will all be there with proverbial bells on."

I am too bone tired to get excited; I hung up, and look for a place to crash.

Chapter Ten -------- Win Lose, or draw?

Wednesday is upon us, and I sleep off and on until the
sun is high and the heat is getting to me. I think I will
sightsee around El Paso City. Moreover, the Marty
Robbins song that grandpa and Dad tried to sing years
ago was the one that grandma rightfully said, Was as
bad as sour owl shit."

Later today I planed on my drive toward Tucson. Toward the cooler evening I began driving yet again.
With all this open country; I wish I could put this old
pickup on automatic pilot. I feel fatigued, as the miles
seem to crawl by and can't help it that my mind con-
jures up yet another obscure scene involving Dad
from the distant past. I remember my very elderly
great-grandmother and her daughter: my Granny visiting for a few days. I believe some kind of large family
reunion was taking place. Also by chance two of my
very young male cousins were spending the night with
us. They must have been about three and four years of
age. I remember Dad saying he had gotten up around
six A.M., and saw these thin twin trails all over the
house. He retraced, and they lead to the bedroom
where the little boys were sleeping. He even checked
to see if they were breathing since he wondered if

food poisoning had caused this severe case of the Hershey squirts. Then he got down on all fours, and he was vigorously wiping the floors and scrubbing our carpets when great-grandma saw him and kept saying,

"Naymen, nay men."

When everything was reconstructed it was discovered that great-grandma was missing from her purse her old chocolate candy-looking laxative. I drove for hours into the night and then after getting into Tucson; I took a series of catnaps in the old pickup. I appropriately continued conjuring recollections of Dad, and I hope it is a good omen. Later this fine afternoon I relaxed in a Tucson air-conditioned restaurant. I avoided reading the newspapers, because my subconscious is in overdrive, and the dye is cast as I am now almost finally there. I do have some silly thoughts, as in if I had never heard this town pronounced, and I looked at the spelling; I would pronounce it Tuxson. Moreover, now my mind wanders back to yet another of Gramps stories. He told me he only went through the eighth grade, but he later read a lot. In addition, he took some correspondence courses. I remember he bragged about how effective they were, but one time he was having an intellectual conversation with a high level sort at a large company he was working for at a menial level job. Gramps had mentioned to this high-up feller a couple times he should put together a resume. The problem was; he pronounced it like start up again or continues on. Gramps said after trying to sound so smart he felt like crawling in a hole after the big shot gave him a wrinkled nose look, and he said, " Do you mean resume," but pronounced it in more of a two syllable French way, rés-umé like it ought a been. Now my mind is flooded with an image from one of Grandpa's old scrapbooks where a Monk in Vietnam had soaked their robe in gasoline, and they just sat on the ground yoga like and lit themselves on fire. They seemed oblivious to the flames, but they seemed to manage to make sure an A.P. cameraman was in the area to film it for posterity.

Now I somehow attract, as I am known to do, attention from a weathered middle aged gent. He just may be nipping a little vodka or something today. We are soon exchanging off-color stories and general information. He comes up with yet another yarn that since I'm from Minnesota and the border of North Dakota where General Custer spent some of his career at Fort Abercrombie that he needed to expand my knowledge of history. He asked me if I knew that Custer had also spent some time right here in Arizona. He could see I didn't realize that, and he tells me Custer quite often liked to go off with a favored gun bearer for a day of hunting wild game. Also that in todays politically correct climate he couldn't divulge the ethnicity of this favored gun bearer. The man continued to say:
Anyway, as Custer is wheeling around to get a shot at a close by fleeing antelope or something, that he by accident, mortally wounds this poor fellow. Custer

genuinely feels bad as he cradles the dying gun bear-
er, but promises the man he will name a new town
springing up in the distance in his honor, so just tell
him a name. The man with his last breath uttered Yu-
ma-----."

I drove up into some beautiful; yet higher country. It is
a little cooler, and I hope conducive to some overdue
earnest prayer. I have a case of those damned mixed
emotions again, as I decided that I better start my final
70 or so mile trip to Tombstone with a good cushion
of time so I'm rested and my reflexes are primed.

Chapter Eleven---------------Interlude with Julie

For years I had such a thing for Carl. I always just knew he would someday see me as a worthy companion. Now that I am carrying his child; I hope with every fiber in my body nothing happens to him at this Friday. Oh, God please help things work out. Does he have a gun; will he be hurt or killed? Oh I hope and pray we will be together; why all this now? Everything will be fine; I must keep telling myself that he will get through this, and we will be together; and we will have a life. I can't wait to see him. I can't wait to tell him how I love him and how I have loved him for so long. My dream came true to be with him, and the moon and the stars must have been just right; I just didn't mean to become pregnant! Oh my God; It is what it is, and I must be strong now.

Chapter Twelve--------------- Here at Last, Here at Last

I guess I actually am here late on Thursday evening. Moreover, some kind of speech or whatever keeps entering my mind as I shorten some pant legs and locate a bungee strap for a make shift belt. I set my trusty wind up alarm for 10:00 A.M., and I hope for some needed shut eye. I sleep off and on into the early morning. I wake up, and I get going even before my alarm sounded. Next, I stopped at a service station to wash off some grime, slip into my gear, and I put on a loose fitting shirt. I wonder if they still have an Alhambra Saloon. I don't have to drive around long before I see a village of television remote trucks with their antennas aimed skyward. I laugh as I think an A.P. Photographer or two might show. It is still some before 11:00 A.M. and I try Chad's cell number.

Chad answers and he said, "Tom, why didn't you call earlier?"

I don't say anything except my location. Yet again the Bon Jovi lyrics come to me but as gramps used to say

I am prepared any old way the mop flops.

Chad is here in a flash, and he is so excited that I have to settle him down.

Chad tells me:

Tom, get in my vehicle, we invited the F.B.I. under-

standably late, and I informed them they should show,
as we hope this can be a cleansing thing for all parties
and the whole nation in effect. Tom we took it upon
ourselves to be you, and I wrote a mission statement
explaining your mindset that day and ensuing actions,
as we realize, it would take considerable time and ef-
fort on your part today, so give it an earnest look, and
sign off on it, so we can print and handout fifty or so
copies to the large media presence here today as soon
as possible. Tom, can you eat some humble pie today
if they swallow some crow with the right garnish-
ment?"

I answered, "Chad, I want to apologize and I plan to
before getting to the what and why of Murphy's Law
that fateful day."

Chad shows some clearance card and he drives thru
throngs of people. He stops, and he pulls me into an
enclosed tent-like structure, and says, "Relax kid, you
are not on for a good twenty minutes."

I questioned, "Chad, do I look nervous?"

Chad answered, "No, and that concerns me."

It seems like only five minutes have gone by when
wow; Professor Vox and Chad come in to lead me out
of a flap that led up some steps to an outside stage.

I am handed a wireless microphone and commence:
My name is Carl Hanson, Jr. and I have come to the
O.K. Corral today to stand up for the future of fair-
ness and justice throughout our great fifty United
States of America. Could I take the liberty of a short

prayer here today? Dear Lord, we pray to you and
everyone for forgiveness, and I have also forgiven any
transgressions toward me, and hope at a minimum, to
get it from you father. I also want to thank everyone
that believed in me, and the people for the print out
today, that attempts to give you some background to
the Murphy's Law nightmare scenario that brings us
together this day.

I then put my heart into retelling the event. My God,
Julie's even here, and she runs up and hugs me. The
whole world must see she is in a family way.

Now I get into my finish, "You will never know how
much I wish I had stayed at the keg party that night."
We all got some needed comic relief from that statement.

I continued, "I am not an expert, or I wasn't one, but
have come to a conclusion, through much thought,
that our Country needs an independent task force or
commission to evaluate and make sure this doesn't
happen again, and if that doesn't get results there will
be a movie or I'll sue the bastards! Thank You and
God Bless."

Now I am glad to see the F.B.I. has sent an apparently
high level dude here today. He introduced himself,
"My name is Bill Gentry and as a representative of the
F.B.I. we had put together a position paper or speech. I
have now taken it upon myself to throw the dam thing
away."

By God he throws some papers over his head, and the

people are laughing and really carrying on.

Gentry continues:

I with the authority vested in me by the F.B.I. fully concur with what Carl junior just said, and we will aggressively act and immediately follow thorough with constructive actions. Today we also wish to announce the lifting of Military Combatant Status of Carl Hanson Senior. We can do a better job, and we will as we have learned from this unfortunate incident

He motions me over, and he gives me; I feel a sincere embrace. He now leans away while still giving me a bear hug.

"Congratulations Carl, for making the best of a nightmare scenario and fighting the good American-spirit fight."

I now lean toward him and whisper, "I am looking forward to the enlightening public trial."

He whispers back, "Come on now junior, we both know that won't be necessary; and nice pants." *We* now both hold our hands up and repeat, "God bless America."

Is this an end point and does the young couple deserves on balance to live happily ever after? I am a bit biased but hope so. Turn the page for an alternative ending if you so please.

Alternative Ending

Wow, I pinch myself as I'm back at Dad's place without the weight of the world on my shoulders. Dad will finally be back home in a promised three days. Julie is busy with sis and their labor of love, pursuing wedding plans, dates and all that stuff, while I make progress on soon getting my delayed College Degree. Life is good!

Two faithful days later

Extra--Extra-- Read all about It-- as the newspaper hawkers or kids selling papers yelled back when junior's Granddad was a kid.

There were some brazen home invasion robberies and in the same neighborhood a botched home robbery where a shooting took place early last evening in Moorhead Minnesota. The victim is in critical condition but apparently he had fired back and wounded at least one of the two accomplices, as there is a blood trail. Authorities strongly state there will be an aggressive investigation.